Teacher with a Tin Star

Mark Brown is hoping to become a minister of the church, but for now he is teaching the elementary school in the little town of Barker's Crossing in Wyoming.

When a local landowner begins to terrorize the home-steaders around Barker's Crossing, Brown realizes that it is time to act. He has not always been a teacher; in fact he was a lawman for over ten years.

Now, before he can fulfil his ambition of becoming a minister, he must take up his gun one last time and fight to defend the helpless.

Teacher with a Tin Star

Harriet Cade

 A Black Horse Western

ROBERT HALE · LONDON

ISBN 978-0-7198-1545-4

Robert Hale Limited
Clerkenwell House
Clerkenwell Green
London EC1R 0HT

www.halebooks.com

Typeset by
Derek Doyle & Associates, Shaw Heath
Printed and bound in Great Britain by
CPI Antony Rowe, Chippenham and Eastbourne

CHAPTER 1

The three loafers, leaning on the hitching rail outside the Luck of the Draw saloon, marked the approach of the town's teacher with undisguised and contemptuous amusement.

'Here comes the schoolmarm!' observed one, in a voice loud enough to be heard by the object of his ridicule. Whether Mark Brown noticed these unflattering words, it was impossible to say.

The school teacher was a nondescript and colourless character, who might have been any age from twenty-five to forty. In fact, he was thirty-one that year. He invariably dressed in sober and semi-clerical black, which tended to confirm the rumour that he intended to take holy orders in the not-too-distant future. For now though, he was superintending the education of the young folk in the town of Barker's Crossing; a small place of just over 500 souls in the north of the Wyoming Territory.

As the teacher drew nigh to them, the men lounging around outside the saloon greeted him politely enough, but with an ironic edge to their voices, suggestive of suppressed laughter.

'Afternoon, Mr Brown.'

'Hey there, Teacher.'

'How's it goin', sir?'

Brown acknowledged the men pleasantly, with a smile and a nod. After he had passed them, but before he was entirely out of earshot, one of the men said emphatically, 'I'd sure hate to be an old maid in britches like that.'

Mark Brown had grown used to the mockery of some of the rougher elements in town. Teaching young children was, it was true, a traditionally feminine job and so it was only to be expected that some might find it entertaining to see a man undertaking the task. He had only held the post for a fortnight; hardly long enough for the novelty to have yet worn off. Well, he thought to himself, as he walked away from the saloon, if a little joshing is the worst that I have to endure in this life, I shall be doing very well.

Truth to tell, Brown had a good deal more on his mind than teasing from the kind of inebriated clowns who congregated in and around the Luck of the Draw. If he was any judge of matters, there was serious trouble heading this way and his main concern just then was to make sure that the children for whom he cared were protected from it.

The open country surrounding Barker's Crossing was rapidly being settled by homesteaders lured there by the government's offer of 160 acres of land for any former soldier of the Union Army. The War Between the States had been over for ten years, but many of those who had fought in it, still hadn't found any permanent employment. As the years passed, the attraction of being given a free stretch of farming land increased, until this part of Wyoming was experiencing what amounted to a land rush. For the town, this meant burgeoning prosperity, but there were others for whom the flood of newcomers spelled ruin.

Until the end of the war, this part of the country had been pretty well all open range, with ranchers allowing their cattle to roam freely across the vast acres of grassland. Some of these men had grown rich and powerful from their activities; after all, they had limitless free land and abundant water. Thousands of cattle could be maintained for no cost at all. All that was needed was to round up the herds each spring and brand any calves. Then the homesteaders began to arrive.

At first, these settlers were more of a nuisance than a serious inconvenience. Slowly but surely though, they began to choke off access to the rivers and streams that were so essential to the big ranchers. Their fences and fields meant that the huge herds belonging to the long-established ranches could no longer move freely on the open range. Worse than this was when some of the newcomers began to raise cattle on their own account. The cattle ranchers could see their stranglehold on stock-raising being broken before their very eyes. The wealthier ranchers had found ways to discourage such enterprise, which was what had led to the present state of affairs. It was in connection with this matter that Mark Brown was presently heading out to visit the families of some of his pupils.

Meanwhile, back at the Luck of the Draw, conversation at the bar was turning to pretty much the same topic: namely the trouble between the homesteaders and the most important rancher in those parts, Randolph Parker.

'What d'ye hear 'bout that shooting the other day?' enquired one drinker of the barkeep, 'Think it was Parker's boys?'

'Couldn't say,' said Nathan Dowty, who had been tending the bar at the Luck of the Draw for as long as most anybody could recollect. 'Like as not it was just some fight 'tween those homesteaders. I hear where they're a regular set of libertines and loose-livers. Maybe they was quarrelling over some woman business.'

There was a pause for a few seconds, as the others digested this opinion. Then another man said, 'Mind, they say that the killer was wearing a spook mask. You know, a white sack with holes cut out for they eyes and mouth. Seems a funny way to carry on if'n they just fighting over some woman.'

A man who didn't live in town and looked to be one of the homesteaders came up to the bar and caught the tail-end of this conversation. He said, 'If this is about that murder the night before last, I can tell you men here for now that there was no woman in the case. It was hired killers from that big spread as is owned by Parker. They killed Tom Sadler 'cause he wouldn't allow any cattle across his land to the river. Parker told him he'd live to regret it and so he has.'

This blunt and unequivocal statement left the others feeling a mite uncomfortable and the conversation moved along other channels.

After he had collected his horse from the field behind the livery stable, Mark Brown headed out of town. A number of his pupils were the children of sodbusters living a couple of miles or more from town. They walked in each morning, their parents somehow scraping together the nickels and dimes needed to pay for the schooling. Three miles from Barker's Crossing lived one of the first of the settlers to make a home in this corner of the territory. Terrence McDermott had arrived with his wife and son six years ago and worked his quarter-section for a year, before suddenly and unexpectedly dying of the bloody flux. Everybody had predicted that his wife would up and leave when her husband died, but she had nowhere to go and so, to the amazement and admiration of her neighbours, stayed on and worked the land herself.

Agatha McDermott, known to one and all as 'Cattle Aggie', had been one of the first homesteaders to begin keeping cattle. This had led to friction with Randolph Parker, as it had set a bad example to others thereabouts, who also started acquiring a few steers and entering into competition with Parker. Since many of these people owned the land lining the various water-courses, it did not take a prophet to see that the way things were going. It was the small farmers with their own land who would be the future of farming in Wyoming, rather than men like Parker who relied upon the rapidly shrinking open range for their livelihood.

In the usual way of things, the teacher enjoyed visiting parents like the widow McDermott. Some mothers and fathers didn't seem to give two hoots what their young ones learned, waiting only for the day that the children would be big enough to help around the house or farm. Others though, like Agatha McDermott, knew the value of education and wanted their own children to reach for a better life than they themselves had been able to hope for.

'Good afternoon, Mr Brown!' cried Aggie when she caught sight of the teacher riding up towards her house. She was engaged in washing a large dog of indeterminate breed and ferocious appearance. 'To what do we owe the pleasure?'

Brown dismounted and came a little closer to the farmer before speaking. He said quietly, 'Is your son near at hand?'

'Patrick? Why no, he's gone over yonder to his friend's to play. What's to do?'

'Everybody in town's talking of the shooting over at the Sadler place. I wanted to speak to you about it without frightening your boy. I'm guessing it had something to do with Parker?'

Mrs McDermott grimaced. 'It's a bad business. Tom Sadler got sick to death o' having Parker's men and steers trampling over his crops. He told Parker straight that he wasn't about to see anybody passing o'er his fields again without leave. His wife says that Parker just kind o' shrugged and told Tom as he'd be sorry.'

'It's much as I thought, then. Anybody see who killed him?'

'Only Sally. His wife, you know. She said as two men rode up to their soddie and called on Tom to come out. He was a game one, came straight out with his scattergun at the ready. Didn't help none. Those men just gunned him down as soon as he came out the door. They had masks on.'

Mark Brown shook his head in disgust. He had never been able to abide such beastly tricks. He said, 'I was wondering if you and some of the other families might like to have their children come to stay in town for a spell? Meaning, if you think there's apt to be any more shooting or such like. I could offer them a shake-down in the schoolroom for a while, if it would help.'

'That's right nice of you, Mr Brown,' said Aggie

McDermott, her usually harsh and uncompromising features softening for a moment, 'You're a real friend. It won't answer though, for all that I'm grateful for the offer.'

'It might be safer for your son. . . .'

'Once you start running and hiding from bad men, there's no end to it. I reckon we'll stop here and see it out together. But like I say, I'm mighty obliged to you for the thought.'

It was the same story at all the other little homesteads along the valley that Brown visited. The men and women were very grateful to him for thinking of them, but not one was intending to split up their families that way in the face of trouble. He couldn't say that he blamed them, really. Why should they back down in the face of naked aggression of this sort? If he himself had a family, thought Mark Brown, as he rode back to town, he would like as not refuse to budge an inch himself. Certainly, he would want to keep his children right by his side, just as these folk did. Well, he had tried.

When he had arrived in the Wyoming Territory, two weeks earlier, Mark Brown had been aiming to take a year's break before studying for the ministry. Teaching school seemed like a peaceful way of spending a twelvemonth, giving him the time to reflect upon what he was planning and deciding whether he really had a vocation for the priesthood. The last thing he had reckoned on was stumbling into a situation like this.

Jack Brady, the old man who ran the livery stable, seemed disposed to be chatty when Brown left his mare there after riding out that afternoon. 'Been visiting, Teacher?'

'Keeping in touch with my pupils, Mr Brady.'

'You want some advice?'

'I can see you want to give me some,' smiled Brown, 'Go on, what would you recommend?'

'Steer clear of Main Street today. There's a bunch of new men working for Parker. They've come into town to get liquored up at the Luck of the Draw. Wild-looking crew. I know some of our boys poke a little fun at you, but these fellows might be something else.'

'I appreciate your concern,' said Brown, before bidding the old man good day and setting off in the direction of Main Street.

'Well,' muttered Brady, 'Nobody can say that I didn't warn him.' He was stricken with a sudden spasm of coughing and when he hawked and spat, there was as much blood as spittle in the dirt. He grimaced and went into his office to get the bottle of medicine he had been given by the doctor.

It wasn't quite dark, but judging by the noise coming from the saloon, it was already doing a roaring trade. Many folk in Barker's Crossing had an ambivalent attitude towards the cowboys from Parker's place. On the one hand, they surely were free spenders, throwing their money around like drunken sailors. But then again, they did tend to get a little rowdy at times and most men liked to know that their wives and daughters were safe at home when a crowd of the ranch hands hit town.

As he approached the saloon, Brown heard a short cry of distress from the space between two of the buildings to his left. It sounded like a child's voice, or maybe that of a young woman. Either way, he felt that he should see if any help was needed. He walked briskly into the deeply shaded alleyway and saw two figures struggling at the far end. 'What's going on there?' he called. Receiving no answer, he carried on down the alleyway, to see what was what.

As he came closer, the teacher realized with a shock that the stifled cry had come from a young woman, really little more than a girl, who was being restrained by a rough-looking fellow of perhaps forty. This man, when he caught sight of Brown, said sharply, 'Get the hell out o' here. This ain't your affair!'

'Well,' said Mark Brown mildly, 'I reckon you're wrong about that, friend.'

The other man turned to face the interloper and released his grip on one of the girl's arms as he did so. Lily-May Cartwright later related to her friends in awe what had next happened, hardly able to believe the evidence of her own two eyes. Like everybody else in Barker's Crossing, she had the teacher marked down for a regular sissy.

'That teacher, he just grabbed ahold of that fellow's shirt-front and swung him round,' she told everyone, 'Banged him into the wall and then, 'fore the man knew what was going on, Mr Brown he reaches his hand down right quick and takes the gun from the other fellow's holster and throws it clear out of the way. Then he grabs the man's hair and proceeds to bang his head back and forth hard on the brick wall. Then, when he's knocked him out stone cold, the teacher lets him fall into the dirt and he says, "You just keep your hands off other folk, you hear what I tell you?" I never seed the like!'

Mark Brown felt sick at heart when he had finished dealing with the ruffian. He had sworn never to lose his temper in this way again. There was not the least doubt that the fellow richly deserved a beating, but this was hardly the conduct that one would expect from a man hoping to become a minister. Not for the first time, Brown felt like a rank failure. If he could not even restrain himself while working as an elementary teacher in a little town like this, what hope was there for his future life?

In the meantime, there was the problem of what to do with this girl, whom he now recognized as the big sister of one of his pupils. 'It's Miss Cartwright, isn't it?' he enquired, 'Whatever happened?'

'I was taking a shortcut round back of the stores, when yon fellow jumped me.'

'You know what they say about shortcuts, I suppose?'

'No, what's that?'

'Shortcuts make for long delays.'

'My pa wanted me home before sundown. I was in a hurry.'

'Well, let's see if we can get you home safely now. You live just down the road aways, don't you? I teach your brother, Billy.'

Mr Cartwright was almost incandescent with fury when he heard what had befallen his sixteen-year-old daughter, his immediate impulse being to charge down to the saloon, find the man who had assaulted his child and shoot him on the spot. Brown talked him out of this rash idea and, without going into details, hinted that the man had already been punished to some extent. It was Lily-May who supplied the details and, when she had finished her account, Pete Cartwright looked at the teacher in a different way. He said slowly, 'I've a notion that we was wrong about you, Brown, and I don't mind owning it. Happen you weren't always a teacher?'

Mark Brown smiled. 'No, it's what you might call a recent development, Mr Cartwright. That doesn't signify. I'm glad I could be of assistance.' He stood up to leave.

'I hope that man you felled doesn't take it amiss and come after you,' said Cartwright. 'I'd be sorry to think as me and mine had put you in danger.'

'I'm not afeared of him,' said the teacher quietly, making it sound not like a boast but merely a plain statement of fact.

The atmosphere in the Luck of the Draw was tense. The men from Randolph Parker's ranch were often a little lively when in their cups, but those who had come into town that afternoon were something else again. For one thing, they did not look or behave like cowboys. There were a dozen of them in the saloon and they all of them looked like men who were unused to hard, physical labour. It was noticed that they dressed more like members of some militia than anything else, with military boots and old patrol jackets; not at all like the run-of-the-mill ranch hands who normally came into town from the Parker spread. Then again, there were the accents. These men sounded as though they were from the Deep South; Georgia or Texas, perhaps. All in all, there was something distinctly odd about such men as these fetching up on a ranch in the northern part of the Wyoming Territory.

These were also men who needed plenty of space around them and did not like to be jostled at the bar or even to have others brush against them as they walked past. Any unwanted contact was met with cold and menacing stares.

Still and all, Parker was an important man locally and it was really nobody's business who he was employing up on his own land. Nevertheless, the presence in the saloon of these hard-looking and apparently touchy types made some of the regular customers feel uneasy. As the evening wore on, the uneasiness increased. There was nothing anybody could put a finger on, but the usual patrons began to drift away from the saloon earlier than would generally be the case. Nathan Dowty shook his head gloomily when he realized that pretty well the only drinkers left in the place were Parker's boys. He had a sharp nose for trouble and although there had been no quarrelling or fighting yet, he surely hoped that these men would not be making a habit of drinking in his saloon. They were the kind of folk who made others feel nervous.

CHAPTER 2

News travels fast in a small town and when the children began to trickle into the schoolroom the morning after their teacher had rescued Billy Cartwright's sister from her awkward predicament, every single child appeared to know exactly what had taken place in that alleyway off Main Street. The source of their information was of course Lily-May's young brother, who was basking in the reflected glory of being among the first to discover that Mark Brown was not the soft fellow that everybody thought him to be.

As his pupils arrived, Brown was a little irritated to see that they were staring at him with new respect. Lord, he thought to himself, all it takes to make these little ones regard you as a grand sort of person is to knock somebody down in the street.

'Is it true, sir, that you beat up on one of the men from the Parker ranch?' asked one boy, who was but eight years of age.

'That's nothing to the purpose,' said the teacher repressively, 'We come here to learn, not discuss nonsense of that kind.'

The morning progressed well enough, until about ten, when there was a knock at the door. One of the girls jumped up to open it and Brown saw to his surprise that standing outside was Linton J. Avery.

Linton Avery's position in the town was a strange one. Although he had a house five miles from Barker's Crossing, he was not a homesteader. As a matter of fact, he was a highly educated man; a qualified lawyer who was also a Justice of the Peace. Although a partner in a law firm in Cheyenne, he preferred living out in the wild for a lot of the time. He was a regular visitor to town and often made business trips south. Why he had made his home out on the range was something of a mystery to folk in town. There were those who suggested that Avery was sweet on Aggie McDermott and that it was that which kept him living out there among the farmers.

'May I help you, Mr Avery?' asked the teacher. 'It's about time for recess, so if you want to talk, we can do so privately here.'

'Thank you. I would like a word or two, if quite convenient.'

Brown addressed the class. 'Children, you may go out quietly to the yard now. Quietly, I said, Billy Cartwright. Unless you'd all like to stay in and do some sums instead of playing outside?'

The children grinned openly at this empty threat

and went careering out into the school yard.

'Take a seat, if you please, Mr Avery. How may I help you?'

Avery drew up a chair to the teacher's table and said, 'I've been hearing all about you in the store, this morning. I tell you, Brown, you're the theme of general conversation!'

'People have nothing better to do with their time than talk a lot of foolishness,' said Mark Brown dismissively. 'Tomorrow, they'll be gossiping about something else.'

'But is its true that you took on one of those new boys from Parker's place? The ones that everybody is so worried about?'

'I don't know who it was I dealt with,' said Brown shortly. 'He was making a nuisance of himself to a young lady and so I put a stop to it. It's nothing. Surely that wasn't what you wanted to speak to me about?'

'Well, only in a manner of speaking. You know, things are coming to a head with Parker and his carrying on against those settlers. It's time you people in town took a stand.'

Mark Brown rubbed his chin thoughtfully. 'I've only been here a fortnight, barely that. I wouldn't say I qualify as one of the townspeople yet awhiles. And what d'you mean by "taking a stand?" ?'

'Here's the way of it. Parker has brought a bunch of men up here from Texas. They're little more than mercenaries, hired guns. You heard about Tom Sadler? Well, that's just the start. What's needed in this town is some proper law. Somebody who will stand firm and rally folk hereabouts to put a stop to Parker and his bandits.'

'Why come to me?' asked the teacher bluntly. 'I'm nobody here.'

'You're an educated man, the same as me. If we want to have a sheriff hereabouts, then first we ought to have a town council. I'm asking if you'd sit on something of the sort, if I could get others to join it?'

'I suppose I might. What then, we would engage guns of our own to stop Parker taking over the district?'

'We'd appoint a sheriff, who could then have deputies, maybe raise a posse, if need be. I want to see proper law and order come to this town. Otherwise, Parker will begin throwing his weight around in town, same as he thinks he rules the range.'

'You're a Justice of the Peace, or so I heard. You could just swear in a sheriff yourself, couldn't you?'

'In theory,' said Avery, 'But that'd look mighty high-handed. I'd as soon the town chose somebody for the job.'

After school had finished for the day and he had tidied up the classroom, Brown went for a stroll along Main Street. It must have been as Avery said, because he was met today not with veiled mockery, but smiles and greetings from the men he passed. The story of how the teacher had knocked down one of Parker's hard men had evidently been doing the rounds. Some of the men he passed on the boardwalk cowered away playfully, as though afraid that the teacher was going to attack them. After five minutes of this, he'd had enough and decided to go for a walk in the hills before heading back to his lodgings. He needed time to think.

The idea of a town council was not a bad one, as far as Brown could see. Randolph Parker was certainly flexing his muscles and Avery was right; if they were not careful, then the rancher would soon be trying to lord it over Barker's Crossing, as well as the scattered homesteads which he was determined to see swept away. The teacher just wasn't sure if he felt like putting himself forward as part of all this. It was one thing to tackle one of those men in the way he had done on the spur of the moment, quite another to become an official part of the town by sitting on a council. On balance, he was of a minded to refuse.

Having come to a decision, Brown felt better. He pulled out the silver hunter which he had inherited from his father and consulted it. It lacked only ten minutes to the hour and if he wasn't careful, he would be late for the evening meal.

Miss Clayton was an elderly spinster who rented out the top floor of her house to what she referred to genteelly as 'paying guests'. She was waiting in the kitchen when Brown hurried in from his walk. He went quickly up to his room, splashed a little water on his face, brushed his hair and hoped that he would pass muster.

'I suppose, ma'am, that you'll be asking what I've

been up to, brawling in the street?' said Brown, once the two of them were seated at the table and ready to eat.

'Oh no, Mr Brown,' the old woman assured him, 'I shouldn't dream of doing anything so vulgar. It's nothing to do with me. Besides, Mrs Cartwright has already given me chapter and verse on that subject.'

'You don't sound shocked,' said Brown and to his surprise, Miss Clayton gave what, from a less respectable and refined person, might have been termed a 'snort'.

'Surprised? Why should I be surprised? I knew what type of man you were when first you came to town. I was pretty well counting off the days 'til you cut loose. I'm only surprised you waited so long.'

'Ma'am?' said the teacher, stunned at this unex-pected statement.

'Oh, don't bother with your play acting here, Mr Brown. Putting on a suit of black and walking about looking sober all the time don't change who you are. For all that you're studying to be a man of the cloth, you'll always be of the same brand.'

'I'm not sure that I rightly take your meaning. . . .' began Mark Brown, before the old woman cut in.

'Pah, don't talk to me! You think I didn't have you pegged for a wild one when first I laid eyes on you? I could pretty much tell you your life's history. Soldier in the war is plain enough. What happened when the bugles sang truce? What did you become then? Road agent or lawman?'

24

'I was a lawman for almost ten years.'

'Ah, I thought as much. What about after that?'

'Approached a theological college and they offered me a conditional vacancy next year. In the meantime, here I am.'

Miss Clayton shook her head emphatically. 'That won't answer. Not for a fellow like you. You can hold yourself in for a year or two, but you'll break loose again. I've known others like you. Tried to change, but found that they couldn't alter what they were within. Go back to being a lawman, you'll never make a priest.'

'That's a matter of opinion, ma'am,' he said, a little stiffly. He was far from pleased that this old woman turned out to be the only one in the whole town who had read him for what he was and also a mite ticked off at the casual way that she dismissed his ambitions. 'I reckon there's worse men than me become ministers of God.'

'That's true enough. But you ain't one of them. I'll warrant another couple of months will see you back to carrying a gun again. Sooner than that, most like.'

'I don't think so,' said Brown, determined to bring the conversation to a close. At that very moment, just as though they had been in a play, there came the sound of shooting from the centre of town; first a single shot and then a ragged fusillade of fire. Brown looked up in alarm and then began to stand up.

Miss Clayton said, a wicked gleam in her eye, 'Ah, this is where the knife meets the bone, as we say in these parts. If you're really determined to be a peaceful minister, then I guess you'll just sit right down again and finish your meal. After all, it's none of your affair who's shooting who.'

The teacher froze for a second like a waxwork in a tableau, unable to decided whether he should just ignore the gunfire or go and see if there was some mischief afoot. There was no telling what might be happening on the streets and with no sheriff or other law within a good many miles, it fell to concerned citizens to handle such matters. He stood up completely and said, 'If you'll excuse me, ma'am, I think somebody ought to see what's what.' He took no notice of the satisfied look on the old spinster's' face as she was confirmed in her opinion of him.

At odd intervals over the twenty-four hours since he had struck down the man who had been pestering Billy Cartwright's sister, Brown had wondered whether or not the fellow would make a point of seeking revenge for being knocked senseless. There was little purpose in speculating further about this, because the man concerned now lay stone dead in the middle of Main Street, with a bullet through his head.

'What happened?' Brown asked one of the group of bystanders surrounding the body.

'A row, over yonder in the saloon. Couple o' Parker's men accused this 'un of cheating at play. He's one of the same crew. They traded blows, then pulled their pistols. Started shooting in the Luck of the Draw, and then it kind o' spilled out here.'

'I guess,' said the teacher slowly, 'That this man was asking for trouble and he found it.'

'That ain't the whole story though,' said another man, 'See over by the general store?'

Brown looked towards the row of wooden buildings and noticed that the front window of the store had been shattered. He was about to remark that a broken window wasn't that serious, when a group of four men emerged from the store, carrying a door on which was laid a body.

'Old man Chivers was just tending his store and peering out the window when a stray ball took him in the chest.'

'Don't tell me he's dead as well?' asked Brown.

'Yep. Two men killed and all over a game of cards. It's the hell of a thing. Never seen the like in this town.'

'What's being done about it?'

The other men in the little group looked curiously at the teacher. They didn't say it out loud, but the unspoken opinion hung in the air between them: what's it got to do with the town's teacher, a man who hasn't lived here more than a few weeks? At length, one of them said, 'Don't know as there's much to do. Chivers was killed by accident and we'll never know whose bullet hit him. Maybe Mr Parker up at the ranch will make some provision for his widow. . . .'

'Do I understand that you're prepared to let this business go?' asked Mark Brown sternly. 'An innocent man gunned down while minding his store and bullets

27

flying round the streets where they might have killed any man, woman or child?'

The others didn't take kindly to being bated in this way and one said, 'What would you have us do, Teacher?'

'This is murder. Somebody was shooting at one man to kill him and shot another while doing so. It's as clear a case of murder as I've ever seen. You men don't want to call the killer to account?'

It was as plain as a pikestaff that this straight-talking was not endearing Brown to the other men and he turned on his heels in disgust and walked back to Miss Clayton's house. The old woman was sitting in the front parlour, drinking coffee. She called him in and asked what the shooting had been. He told her briefly.

'Yes, it's just as you might expect. That Randolph Parker is bringing in a set of scallywags and scamps. It's no wonder that there's been trouble. What are you planning on doing about it?'

'Me? Why should I be doing anything? I have my hands full teaching those children.'

'You stand there and tell me that you've not been itching over the last day or two to step in and put a stop to some of the goings-on that you've seen in this district since you arrived?'

'I don't belong here, Miss Clayton. It's not for me to put myself forward.'

'You'll wait then 'til Parker has driven off all those farmers and then starts to lean on Barker's Crossing and bend that to his will as well?'

A little nettled by her sharp tone, Brown said, 'If you must know, ma'am, I have it in mind to do what I should have done a while back. Tomorrow, I'm going to ride over to Parker's place and tell him that he ought to back off a little and leave folk alone.'

Miss Clayton smiled. 'Ah, that's more like it. And what'll you do if he tells you to clear out and tend to your own affairs?'

'I'll reason with him,' was all that Mark Brown would say further, before bidding the old woman goodnight.

CHAPTER 3

Randolph Parker had been running his herds across the range here for over twenty years now. He had begun his ranch ten years before the Wyoming Territory had even come into existence. He had been here since this land was officially designated as part of the Louisiana Purchase, watched as it became the Nebraska Territory and then seen its name changed to the Dakota Territory. Seven years ago, the name had been changed again, into the Wyoming Territory and it was about then that the trickle of hopeful settlers began to arrive on his land. Because Randolph Parker regarded all the wide acres on which he grazed, his cattle as being his land, he had come here before any of them. Built his house, raised his family and hung on there through those difficult early days. Hung on, until now he was one of the richest men for many miles around. And now, everything that he had worked and fought for was being cast into hazard.

Every day, the squatters and nesters were making

his life more and more difficult. Already, his herds were having to travel fifteen or twenty miles to find unobstructed access to water, and the fences going up all over this part of the country were reducing the area available for the steers to eat. Not this year, maybe not next year or the year after that, but certainly within five or ten years, the range would have disappeared entirely and his ranch would be hemmed in and surrounded by little dirt farmers, grubbing for a living on his land. Well, not while Randolph Parker had breath in his body, they wouldn't!

Hiring those men from the south had been the first gambit in a campaign which would eventually bring this whole district under his control. It was no good fighting one little battle here, driving one man off the land there; he needed to assert his authority over the range and the town both, once and for all. If there would be bloodshed, then so be it. He hadn't sought this trouble, but he was damned if he would back down from it now that it had arrived.

On the morning after the killing of old Chivers, the store-keeper, Parker was standing outside his massive, stone-built house. He was admiring a strange contraption which had been put together on his instructions over the last week or so. It was a wooden hut, little bigger than a toolshed, carried on the back of a specially adapted cart with a ramp at the back which could swing down. Although it was so small, the hut had two neat windows cut at the front and looked for all the world like a giant-sized doll's house.

31

'That will do just fine,' said Parker to the men who had brought the structure for his approval, 'We can start using it this very day. Go and plant it by the stream running by Sadler's fields. You can take it in turns to sleep there until we stake our claim. I don't see Sally Sadler trying to stop you.'

'How long we got to leave it there?'

'No more than a week. Once I register the claim, we'll move it on.'

Parker had come up with this new tactic just recently. In addition to scaring off the settlers by the occasional killing, he had decided to try and tie them up in legal disputes; court cases for which he had the time and money and they did not. One of these was to set down this wooden cabin on somebody else's land and file a claim. Then, if there was an argument about the matter, he would get his lawyer in Cheyenne to fight the case. In the meantime, he would treat the 160 acres surrounding his little shed as being his own land, to do with as he wished. In this way, if his plans went well, Randolph Parker would, little by little, be returning the cultivated land around his ranch to open range.

As this conversation came to an end, Parker spotted a lone rider coming along the drive leading to his property. It was a man dressed entirely in black and for a moment, he felt uneasy, as though the man coming towards him might be a harbinger of misfortune. Then he saw that it was only the teacher from town and he laughed at his misgivings.

'Good morning to you, Teacher,' said Parker, as

Mark Brown rode up, 'I hope you're not looking for new pupils here? There's no young'uns on this ranch.' As he said this, he glanced towards his men, who dutifully gave sycophantic sniggers at their boss's wit.

'What I wished to see you about has no reference to education,' replied the other gravely. 'I wonder if you could favour me with a few minutes of your time?'

The rancher stared at Brown for a few seconds, unable to figure out the play. Then he said, 'Come into the house.'

Parker's house looked to Mark Brown more like an expensive whorehouse than the inside of a normal home. Everywhere he looked, there was red plush, pier-glasses and more vases and etchings than he had ever seen outside of a gallery. This, he thought, is what happens when a man with no taste at all gets hold of too much money.

'Make yourself at home,' said Parker in a friendly enough fashion. 'I know it's early, but would you care for a drink?'

'Coffee or soda water would be nice. Thank you.'

A servant brought in a huge, solid silver coffee pot and once their cups had been filled and the woman had retired from the room, Parker said, 'Well, what's to do?'

'I've come about the shooting in town last night. You heard about it?'

'I heard. What of it?'

'I was wondering what you were fixing to do about it?'

'Do?' asked Parker, a note of amusement in his voice, 'Do? What do you think I should do?'

'The men who carried out those killings are employed by you. I'd say as that gives you some responsibility to act.'

'Employed by me, were they? Well now, that's a horse of another colour. What are their names?'

'I don't know their names.' admitted Brown.

'Why do you think they were from my ranch?'

'There's a bunch of men, Southerners, who you've recently engaged. They were part of that crew.'

Randolph Parker laughed out loud at that. 'You know more than I do then. Sure, I have a few boys from Texas. I got cowboys here from all over the Union. You say that some of my men were mixed up in a shooting at Barker's Crossing. Well, I'm a law abiding man. Give me the details and I'll do what any other man in my position would.'

There was an uncomfortable pause, before the teacher got to his feet and looked down thoughtfully at Parker. He said, 'I won't fox with you, Mr Parker. It's enough that you know I'm on to this. Leave those homesteaders alone and don't send your bullies into town.'

Without moving from the leather armchair, Parker said, 'For a teacher, you're taking an awful lot upon yourself. What are you about?'

'Like I say, Mr Parker, just leave folk be and look after your own ranch. I can see myself out.'

After the teacher had gone, Parker went out to his

men and said, 'Anybody know anything about that fellow?'

'The teacher? They say in town as he's a bit of a sissy. Quiet type, never seed him yet in the saloon.'

Another man said, 'Why, boss? You want that we should deal with him?'

'Maybe. Let's see how things pan out over the next week. Get that hut over to Sadler's fields now and set it down by the stream. Johnson, you can stay there tonight.'

The first person Brown saw when he got back to town was Linton Avery. He hailed him and then dismounted, the better to have a private chat with the fellow. 'Any success with your town council plan?' he asked.

Avery shook his head and said, 'I haven't asked all those I'd like to see on it, but so far not one man will take part. They all think that if they just sit tight, those problems on the range will pass 'em by.'

'I'll do it,' said the teacher suddenly, 'I'll be on your council.'

'Good man! Well, it's a beginning.'

Many schools ran on Saturday mornings as well, but Brown didn't like to see children cooped up in the classroom for too long. The way he saw it, running around in God's open air would do their bodies good and that was every bit as important as their minds. As he walked down the street, he bumped into various of his pupils, all of whom greeted him cheerfully. The teacher fancied that the adults he saw were a little more polite to him as well. It was strange how hearing that a man had been mixed up in a rough-house could alter so many people's view of him! He was, after all, the same fellow he had been before he knocked down that scoundrel. Then he recalled that the man was dead now and felt that he owed him a little respect. Still and all, a scoundrel was what he had been in life.

While he was musing in this way, Brown nearly bumped into a young man who was standing right in front of him, blocking the boardwalk. 'Sorry, fella,' he said, as he made to walk round the youth, 'My fault entirely, I was miles away.'

'Oh, I was waiting for you, you sir. My name's Andy.'

'Andy? That doesn't bring anybody to mind. Do I know you?'

'No, Mr Brown, but my great aunt, Miss Clayton, that is to say, told me as you wanted my help.'

'Help? What do'you mean? Help in the school-room?'

'No, sir. Aunt Jemima said that you might need somebody who could shoot straight. I'm the best shot in town.'

'I don't understand this conversation at all,' declared Mark Brown. 'Why would a teacher need somebody who could shoot straight? I'm not aiming to keep control of the classroom by gunfire. Lord, I don't even strike those children, let alone shoot 'em.'

The young man, who could not have been older than sixteen or seventeen, moved a couple of paces closer to the teacher and lowered his voice. 'I think my aunt has the idea that you are going to be doing something other than teaching before too long.'

'Well it's news to me. Tell me, does your aunt Jemima often,' Brown hunted around for a more polite expression than 'poke her damned nose into other people's business', and finally came up with, 'Take such a lively interest in other folk's affairs?'

'Oh yes, sir. Most all the time.'

'Well, Andy, if I should find the need for a sharp-shooter, I promise I'll keep you in mind. But I wouldn't cancel any other plans you might have. It's apt to be a long wait 'til I call on your services.'

It was almost midday and so the teacher headed back wrathfully to Miss Clayton's house. He was ready to eat, but also wanted to say a word or two to the old lady about her interference. Telling her young nephew that he needed a gunman, indeed! He'd never heard the like.

'Is that you, Mr Brown?' called Miss Clayton, as he entered the house. 'Food will be on the table directly. You might come to the kitchen and lend me a hand with the plates.'

As he entered the kitchen, Brown saw to his surprise that Linton Avery was standing there, chatting to Miss Clayton. 'You must have fairly run to get here before me, Mr Avery,' said the teacher. 'I wasn't aware that you two knew each other.'

'Oh, we're old connections,' said the other man casually. 'What's this I hear about you being a lawman in the past? You kept that quiet.'

'I had my reasons.'

The three of them sat down to what was, for Mark Brown at least, a rather uncomfortable meal. He felt himself to be in somewhat of a false position and was regretting having confided in Miss Clayton about his past life. Once they began eating, Avery turned to him and said, 'I'll take oath you can guess what I'm going to ask you.'

'Truth to tell, Mr Avery, I haven't had much use for guessing games since I was a small child. You got something to say, then you'd best just come out straight with it.'

'Go on,' urged Miss Clayton, 'Just ask him.'

'I thought that you might want to be sheriff of this town, if we can get some sort of agreement, that is. I don't believe that we've got anybody in town who actually knows anything about the business. I reckon you'd be a shoo-in for the post.'

'It's not to be thought of!' exclaimed Brown. 'After a little more time spent teaching here, I'm going to train for the ministry. I'm not using a gun again.'

'He don't mean it,' chipped in the old woman, 'You'll see, he'll change his mind yet.'

'I'd be mighty obliged to you, ma'am,' said Brown, turning to her, 'If you would leave me to speak for myself. And while we're on the subject, what made you tell your nephew that I'd want his shooting abilities?'

'I did?' asked Miss Clayton in surprise. 'Did I? Well, I might've done at that. Well, if you are going to be sheriff, I suppose you'll want a deputy or two. You could do a sight worse than young Andy.'

'Yes, but I ain't going to be sheriff. You know fine well that in another few months, I'll be studying for the ministry.'

'Oh, that!' said the old woman with infinite scorn, 'I already told you, that won't come off.'

'Tell me,' asked Brown curiously, 'Why are you so set on seeing me as sheriff here? Don't you like church ministers?'

'I like 'em well enough. It's just that you wouldn't make a very good one. You'd only ever be fair to middling. I'll warrant you make a top-notch lawman though. I don't like to see a man waste the talents as the Lord has given him.'

Between the shrewd businessman and the opinionated old lady, Mark Brown felt that in another moment he would be signing up as sheriff of Barker's Crossing, just to shut the pair of them up. As it was, Linton Avery said, 'Ah, leave the fellow alone now. He'll come round in his own good time.'

'As for you, Mr Avery,' said Brown, goaded now to the point where he felt like speaking plainly and not mincing his words, 'I reckon you're playing some game of your own. You want a sheriff to stop Parker leaning on your fancy woman out there on the range, maybe.'

There was a silence and then old Miss Clayton laughed. 'He's got you there, Linton, and no mistake.'

'I'll tell you this, both of you. I won't be made any man's cat's paw. I'll do what I will for my own reasons, not to oblige another or fit in with his plans. And I tell you now, there isn't the least hope of me being sheriff here.'

Which was funny, really, because the very next day, Mark Brown was knocking on Avery's door, telling him that he was dead set on becoming the sheriff of Barker's Crossing.

CHAPTER 4

Two things happened the day after Brown had that awkward meal with Miss Clayton and Linton Avery. The first was that the teacher heard about the conduct of the Texans working for the Parker ranch. They were beginning to lean on the tradesmen in Barker's Crossing; taking goods and then suggesting that they be given credit. A couple of them pulled this trick in the general store and made off with thirty dollars' worth of stuff. Nobody present wanted to be the one to challenge the men as they left with their booty and the owner knew that he would be unlikely ever to see a cent for the things they had taken.

Nathan Dowty found himself in difficulties as well, when some of the Southerners who had taken to hanging out in the Luck of the Draw offered to act as his helpers in dealing with any fighting or other trouble which might erupt in his saloon. He tried to explain that there was seldom any trouble in the place and that he didn't really need any help, but they reminded him of the recent shooting. It took a time for the coin to drop, but in the end, Dowty realized that he was being made the victim of a racket, whereby these men would undertake to behave themselves if they and their friends were guaranteed free drinks all night. The question was left open, but he could see that those men would either drink the place dry for free or smash up his saloon to punish him for not giving in to their demands.

Mark Brown heard about these events as he walked to and from church the next day, but by themselves, they would not have been enough to make him change his mind about becoming more involved in the town's future. That was all to change, later that day, when he went for his Sunday afternoon constitutional and chanced to see Sally Sadler and her two young children coming into town on an ox wagon. The young woman was having difficulty in getting the ox to do as she wanted and so Brown called out, 'Need any help there?'

'Oh, could you? The beast has just stopped dead and won't move.'

They introduced themselves and when he heard her name, the teacher said, 'I was right sorry to hear of your loss, Mrs Sadler. Will you be holding the funeral here in town?'

'We had it yesterday. I thought it right to bury Tom on his own land. If I'd known though. . . .'

'Known what, if you don't mind me asking? Here, if you'll allow me, I'll hop up on to that there seat and endeavour to show your ox just who is in charge.'

'Don't start moving yet,' said the young widow. 'I'd like to tell somebody about last night. I was minded to stop right where we were, even with my husband dead. Like Aggie McDermott, you know. But I surely can't now.'

'What happened?'

'Yesterday, some of Parker's boys fetched up on our land. They had a wood cabin on the back of a wagon and dumped it down by the river. I asked what they were about, but they just laughed at me.'

'This cabin. Was it about seven foot high, with two little windows at the front?'

'Yes, how d'you know that?'

'Called on Randolph Parker yesterday and saw it there in front of his house. I wondered what was afoot. Go on.'

'Last night, as we lay in bed, I heard somebody outside our soddie. Maybe there was more than one. Anyways, it was men. They was whispering a lot of dirt, saying what they would do to me if I stayed there another night. I got these little ones to care for, I can't take the risk. So here I am.'

'Meaning that now Parker has a claim to your land, on account of he has somebody living on it and you've given up your own claim by leaving.' The teacher said this more to himself than to the woman at his side, as though he were ravelling a thread out loud.

'I never seed it so,' said Mrs Sadler. 'You think I was wrong to leave?'

'I don't say so. I think any woman in your position woulda done the self-same thing.' Brown shook the reins viciously and succeeded in getting the ox to start moving in the direction of Barker's Crossing.

After he had safely manoeuvred the ox cart into town, Mark Brown jumped down and went off to the church, which was empty now until the evening service. Once inside, he settled down in a quiet corner and prayed for guidance.

'Lord,' he said, 'Seems to me like there's a heap of things need dealing with in this town and folk being pushed about. I know you hate to see the widow and orphan being mistreated, or so I apprehend from reading the Book of Amos, and I have seen such goings-on this very day. I can't sit idly by while there are such goings-on, so I hope you'll understand if I feel as I have to set this right before I can start serving you properly as a minister of your church.'

Having received no reply from the Deity, the teacher stood up and left the church. He wasn't at all sure whether he was doing the right thing, but if nobody else was going to act on behalf of the weak and vulnerable, then he supposed he would be compelled to do so himself.

When he got back to the house, Miss Clayton was sitting quietly, sipping a cup of coffee. She invited Brown to join her, which he did.

'Is your friend, Mr Avery, in town today?' he enquired.

'Not that I'm aware of,' replied the old woman,

'Why, did you want to see him?'

'I have a little business to talk over with him, that's all.'

'You must be right vexed with us after chivvying you about yesterday?'

The teacher laughed. 'No, not really, ma'am. I'm old enough to take care of myself. If a couple o' folk want to badger and pursue me, I reckon I'll live. 'Sides which, you might have a point.'

'Oh?'

'I came across Tom Sadler's widow on the road out of town. You recall that man as was murdered a few days ago?'

'I remember it well enough,' said the old woman grimly.

'Seems like she's had to leave her own land on account of Parker's men. Time that sort of thing was halted.'

Later that day, Mark Brown went down to the livery stable to collect his mare from the field there. Old Mr Brady said, 'Goin' out to see more o' your pupils?'

'Not exactly.'

'You play your cards close to your chest, don't you?'

'It's just that news travels so fast in this town, I'm afraid to tell anybody what I'm doing. It's nothing personal.'

'I ain't about to start a gossipin'.'

'Well, then, I'm off to see Linton Avery.'

The old man looked at him hard. 'You goin' to join this famous town council as he's talkin' of? Wouldn't have thought you were the type for committees and councils and all that foolishness.'

'Why d'you say that?'

'Just the way you have with you.'

As he rode out of town, Brown wondered again if he was doing the right thing. It had now been two months since he had quit being a marshal and if he was honest with himself, he did miss some parts of the work. But after the last shoot-out in which he was involved, he had been so sickened at the slaughter, that he had firmly resolved to lay down his gun for good. Not only that, he honestly believed that the Lord had called him into His service. It was to test whether or not he had a genuine vocation that he had come out here to this little town and taken a humble job, serving those little ones that the Lord so loved.

Most of the homes out on the grasslands were no more than simple soddies; low, single-storey buildings with the walls made of cut turf. Avery's house was a little different, though. He had paid somebody to haul a lot of cut timber out here and build for him a neat little house that wouldn't have looked out of place in New England. It had even been painted white. Brown had heard somewhere about a French Queen, Marie-Antoinette, was it? Any way, this woman had played at being a shepherdess, dressing up for the part and even spending time in a quaint, rustic hut. Something about that story reminded him of this attorney, living out here on the range and pretending to be a settler. Not for the first time, Brown wondered what Avery's game was.

Linton Avery appeared pleased to see the younger man. 'Come right in, Mr Brown,' he said, when he opened the door. 'Will you have a drink?'

'Coffee would be nice, if you have any. Thanks.'

As he pottered about in the tiny kitchen, Avery called out, 'What brings you out here? More than just a social call, I'll be bound.'

'You might say so.'

'Well, out with it, man,' said Avery, as he brought in a tray with the coffee pot, cups and saucers and milk jug on it. 'You'll find it good policy with me to state your case plainly, with no shilly-shallying.'

'The way you do?' asked Mark Brown laconically, which provoked a gale of laughter from his host.

'I like you, Brown. I really do. Well then, what can I do for you?'

'Is it true that you're a Justice of the Peace?'

'That's true enough. Why d'you ask?'

'You can solemnise marriages and suchlike, bury folks too and issue 'em with certificates of birth?'

'Yes, yes, get to the point, man. I don't want to be chasing round the woodpile all afternoon.'

'And you can swear in sheriffs as well?'

'Yes, of course. . . .' Avery said impatiently, then stopped and stared at the teacher in astonishement. 'My God, you want me to swear you in, so you can take down Parker.'

'Let's take it a step at a time. You can swear in a peace officer?'

'I can do it in an emergency and then seek to get the thing confirmed later, yes.'

Mark Brown said nothing more for a space, just sipping his coffee and looking out the window. Avery said, 'Mind, I'd need to know somewhat about you, before I could do that. Be sure you were a man of good character and suchlike. Where were you a lawman? Before you turned up here, that is?'

Still the teacher remained silent, as though he hadn't even heard the question. Then he said quietly, 'I started off as a deputy in Springfield, Illinois. Later, I was in Louisville, over in Kentucky. I was marshal there until two months gone. There's plenty as'll vouch for me there, if you can wire the marshal's office.'

'Why did you leave? What caused you to give up a good career like that?'

'Does it matter?'

'I reckon.'

'You want to show me round your place?' asked Brown.

The two men walked round the land surrounding the preposterous little white clapboard cottage. Avery had made no real effort at cultivation. Near the door, he had stuck a rosebush in the ground and a little further off, there were a few stunted twigs which indicated that a hedge around the place had been contemplated at some time. Beyond that, it was just grass as far as the eye could see.

'You never thought to do any actual farming round

here?' asked Brown.

'This is my retreat. I divide my time between here, Barker's Crossing and Cheyenne. I don't really have time for digging and ploughing.'

The teacher stood and gazed towards the horizon. He said, 'You asked why I handed in my badge. Here's the way of it. I was with a few other fellows, trying to rescue a woman and her child who were being held in a bank. We jumped the robbers, see, and they grabbed ahold of this woman and her six year-old daughter. Upshot was, there was a shoot-out and everybody was killed.'

'Was it your fault?'

'No. Young man with me started the shooting. That woman and her little girl were nonetheless dead for that, though.'

'That what made you want to be a man of God?'

'I was that before those deaths. They just made me think o' devoting my life to the Lord.'

'Well, you want me to swear you in, under the powers that I have, I'll do it.'

'Let's get on with it then.'

Back in the house, Linton Avery went to a bureau and took out a sheet of paper. He handed this to Brown, saying, 'I reckon this oath might be familiar to you. It's pretty much the same kind of rigmarole as you went through when you signed up as a peace officer before. Read out the words on this paper.'

'I, Mark Brown, do solemnly swear that I will perform with fidelity the duties of the office to which

I have been elected, and which I am about to assume. I do solemnly swear to support the constitution of the United States and to faithfully perform the duties of the office of sheriff for the Territory of Wyoming. I further swear that I have not promised or given, nor will I give any fee, gift, gratuity, or reward for this office or for aid in procuring this office; that I will not take any fee, gift, or bribe, or gratuity for returning any person as a juror or for making any false return of any process and that I will faithfully execute the office of sheriff to the best of my knowledge and ability, agreeably to law.'

'I have witnessed your oath, this fourth day Of April, in this year of grace eighteen hundred and seventy five. You got a gun?'

'I have. Back at where I'm staying.'

'You brought a gun with you when you came to teach elementary school? You sure you weren't half expecting to slip back into upholding the peace?'

'Not a bit of it.'

'I've got a badge somewhere. I'll hunt it out and then drop it off at Jemima's house for you.'

And so the die was cast. It had, thought Brown, taken him less than a month to sign up again as a lawman. He still hoped to find that he had a vocation for the ministry, but before he could even think on that matter, he would need to sort things out here in Barker's Crossing. It had taken him only a few minutes to be sworn in and it would take even less time for him to hand in his resignation when things were dealt with. Doing a spell of law-keeping didn't signify; it wasn't like he had given up his ambitions in that other and more godly direction.

He passed by Aggie McDermott's house on the way back into town and found that it was a hive of activity. Aggie was wrestling with some calves, trying to separate them from their mothers and get them into a pen. When she saw the teacher, she stopped what she was doing and came over to say hello.

'You must think me a right one, working like this on the Sabbath,' she said, half-jokingly. 'But the roundup starts tomorrow and I want to make sure all my stock are branded. Parker has been known to get a little tetchy about mavericks. The word "rustling" has been bandied about before.'

'You have your own brand registered?' asked Brown, interested. 'I thought that the big stockmen tried to prevent small farmers like you from having their own brand?'

'I guess you know as Parker's head of the WSA, the Wyoming Stockman's Association. They fought tooth and nail to stop any of us small folk having our own brands.'

'You seemed to manage it.'

Aggie McDermott winked at him. 'Helps if you've got a good friend who's also a slick city lawyer.'

'You mean Mr Avery?' Brown felt suddenly embarrassed. 'I didn't mean to pry. . . .'

Aggie roared with laughter. 'I declare, you're blushing. It's no secret about me and Linton.'

'So what is it with these mavericks?' asked the teacher, anxious to change the subject. 'I never really understood what that was all about.'

'It's no great mystery. Every year in the spring, there's a round-up of all the herds on the open range. The boys separate out those belonging to their ranch and then any calves get branded. There's an old tradition that any unbranded calves, what you call mavericks, are fair game for any as want to take them. The big fellows like Parker claim that we are stealing his calves and then pretending they're ours. Most o' the time, it's just a way to stop us having any cattle of our own. That's why they don't want us to have official brands. That way, if we have any steer that's not branded, they can claim that we're rustling.'

Aggie McDermott's son came out of her soddie at that moment, saying, 'Ma, the coffee's ready now.' Catching sight of the teacher, he said, 'Oh, good day, sir. I'm pleased to see you.'

Patrick McDermott was a tall, good-looking boy of eleven. He was the oldest of Mark Brown's pupils and although very well-behaved and polite, it was clear that he thought himself too old to be sitting in the schoolroom. He was just itching for the day that his mother would allow him to become the man of the place around their little farm. For her part, Cattle Aggie was determined that the boy should soak up as much book learning as was humanly possible. She herself had never even been to school and could barely read and write. She had had to fight, every inch of the way, to get where she was now and did not want the boy's life to be a similar grim struggle. She sensed instinctively that the key to his future lay in a sound education.

'Will you come in and set down with us, Mr Brown?' said Aggie, 'And have a coffee?'

'I'd love to, ma'am, but I have urgent and pressing business back in town. Thanks, any way.'

'Urgent business on a Sunday? That don't listen right for a man who's aiming to be a preacher.'

'Recollect that the Sabbath was made for man, not man for the Sabbath.'

And so Mark Brown parted amiably from Aggie McDermott, joshing and laughing. He never saw her again alive and was glad later that his last contact with her had been so good-natured and pleasant.

Back at Miss Clayton's house, the evening was approaching and the old woman was preparing for her second outing to the church that day. When the teacher came through the door, she could see at once that something about him had changed. 'Mr Brown, I wondered where you had got to. Will you be accompanying me to the evening service?'

'I can't, ma'am. I have what you might call a pressing matter to attend to here.'

'More pressing than divine worship? How shocking!' She said this with a twinkle in her eye, to show him that she was only joking.

Brown waited until Miss Clayton had left for church, before going up to his room and hauling his trunk out from under the bed. Linton Avery had been quite right. It was odd that when coming to this town to work as a schoolmaster, he had at the last minute felt impelled to pack his holster and gun at the bottom of all the other things which a teacher might legitimately need when instructing a group of young children.

The teacher removed bundles of papers and books which dealt with various matters relating to education. Beneath those were some rougher clothes than the black suit he always sported since coming to Barker's Crossing. Under those old duds was a bulky package, wrapped in oil cloth. He fished this out of the trunk and then laid it on the bed. As he did so, there came unbidden to his mind, the memory of that last fatal shoot-out in which he had been involved.

The marshal's office had received a tip-off that an attempt was going to be made to knock over the biggest bank in Louisville. They never did find out where this warning had come from, but it sounded like a true bill. Brown and three other men had surrounded the First National Bank before it opened for business that day. The youngest of their party, Abe Miller who was only nineteen, had been hidden in an upper storey of a building overlooking the bank. It had been impressed upon the young man most forcibly that he was under no circumstances to open fire, unless somebody else started shooting first.

Mark Brown himself had been walking up and down the street casually, trying to look like any other citizen. The robbery had begun and then, as the bandits were leaving the bank, Abe Miller had shot at them, in flat defiance of his instructions. The men had darted back into the bank and grabbed the only other customers in there at the time, a mother and her little girl. Everything happened so fast after that, that there really wasn't time for anybody to get up into that second floor office and knock young Miller over the head, so that he couldn't fire again. Ten seconds after the robbers had ducked back into the bank, they came charging out again, with their hostages held in front of them. Abe Miller had shot one of them through the head. It was a fine piece of shooting at that range, Brown had to give the boy that. Only thing was, it triggered a general gun battle as the men tried to make their way down the street to where they had left their horses. They never made it.

Once the firing began, it became a free for all. Since the officers were all firing from cover and the men who had robbed the bank were right there in the middle of the road, it was clear who had the advantage and how it would end. What nobody had bargained for, though, was that in addition to the five outlaws lying dead in the dirt, there would also be a young woman of perhaps twenty-five and her little daughter. Brown had been so angry that he'd marched straight up to Miller and knocked the young man unconscious with his pistol butt. It hadn't brought the little girl back to life, though.

When Miss Clayton returned from church, it was to

find Mark Brown sitting at her kitchen table, in the process of stripping down and cleaning a Colt revolver.

CHAPTER 5

'That's a fine occupation for the Sabbath, I must say,' said the old woman disapprovingly, when she caught sight of the gun. 'I'm glad to observe you've had the kindness to spread some newspaper on the table cloth. I'll thank you not to get any oil stains on it.'

'I'm a neat enough worker when I'm doing aught of this sort,' said Brown, polishing the barrel of the pistol carefully. 'You wouldn't happen to have any bacon fat, I suppose?'

Miss Clayton went into the pantry and returned with a small earthenware pot. 'You'll not be needing much, I guess?'

'A tiny smear is all.'

Fascinated in spite of herself, the old woman sat down at the table opposite Brown. His large hands worked swiftly, oiling and cleaning. He was as deft as a woman with a piece of fine embroidery. 'What do you want with the fat?' she asked.

'Sometimes sparks fly out into the other chambers

when you fire. If you're not careful, you can find your-self firing off two or three shots at once. A little fat round the mouth of the chamber stops sparks getting in.'

'You seem to know your stuff.'

'I'd hope so, Miss Clayton. I've lived by use of my gun since the war began. Signed up the very same day that Mr Lincoln called for volunteers. After Fort Sumter, you know.'

After he had thoroughly cleaned and oiled the pistol, the teacher put it back together again, tapping in the wedge which held the barrel in place with a tiny wooden mallet. Then, after spinning the cylinder a couple of times to make sure that it was running smoothly, he produced a copper powder flask and filled each of the chambers in turn.

'I suppose this all has something to do with my brother-in-law?'

'Your brother-in-law, ma'am? I don't rightly know who you might mean.'

'Linton Avery, of course. Didn't I tell you as he was married to my baby sister, once upon a time?'

'I don't recall that you did.'

'What are you going to do when you've got this weapon all settled nicely?'

Mark Brown didn't answer immediately, but looked as though he was carefully weighing up the question. At length, he said, 'I shall go back and see Randolph Parker. Tell him things have changed since last I saw him. Then I'll ask him to keep his men out of town for a while and to stop trying to steal any more land.'

'You know how to open your mouth wide,' said Miss Clayton admiringly. 'What if he tells you to get lost?'

'I hope he won't. If he does, then he and I are likely to fall out.'

It struck Mark Brown that it would be a shabby trick to abandon his classroom, just because he had taken on another post. All other considerations apart, nothing had been said when he was talking to Avery about where any salary might be coming from if he took up the job of sheriff. And so both ethical and financial motives coincided, and the following Monday morning saw the teacher setting out the schoolroom the same as usual. If he was going to be at outs with Randolph Parker, then there was no earthly reason why it couldn't be after he had finished teaching school that day.

The children were pleased to see him and the morning went pleasantly enough. After he had dismissed school for the midday break, Linton Avery showed up. He said, 'Surprised to find you still teaching the ABC to these children. Thought you might have been planning what to do next.'

'You can leave me to tend to that, Mr Avery. I'll be riding out to Parker's ranch this evening and setting things out plain for him.'

'You'll be needing this then.' Avery took from his vest pocket a small tin star. As he handed it to the teacher, he paused, saying, 'You sure you're up to this, Brown?'

'Don't you worry none. This is business that I know about.'

After school had finished, Brown went home and took out of his trunk a holster and belt. It was not a gunslinger's fancy rig, nor anything like. In fact, it was nothing more elaborate than an old artillery holster, with the strap at the top cut off and most of the holster also cut away, so that only the barrel of the pistol was held secure. The belt was an old one as well; intended not to hold up Brown's pants, but to keep the holster at such a height as to allow the hilts of the pistol to brush easily against the inside of his forearm, halfway between elbow and wrist.

Once he had strapped on the holster, he took the pistol out of the trunk and added that. He felt complete again, in a way he had not done for several months. Then he pinned the star to his jacket and stood in front of the looking glass hanging above the wash-stand. Well, thought Mark Brown, I have had a deal of fun teaching those children and there's no denying it. Still and all, a job of work like this present one is more in my line.

Old Miss Clayton arrived back home, just as Brown was leaving. When she set eyes on him, she all but gasped. 'Well, I'll say you don't look much like a teacher any more. You think as you'll be able to straighten this trouble out for us, Mr Brown? Those Texans are behaving like they own the town today. Think you can handle them?'

'We'll have to see, ma'am. I've dealt with some

rough customers in my time.'

It was a fine spring evening when the new sheriff rode up the drive to Randolph Parker's ranch. The man himself wasn't present, but one of his boys gave directions to a spot about a mile from the house, where he said his boss would be found. He looked uneasily at Brown, noting the gun and badge. As soon as Brown had set off in search of Parker, this man hurried off to find some of the new boys and tell them that Brown was heading off after the man who they were pledged to protect.

Randolph Parker was in a clearing in a little wood, directing a team of men who looked as though they were building a miniature log cabin. There was so much shouting and swearing that nobody heard him ride up. It wasn't until one of the men spotted him and went over to alert Parker, that the work halted and those present gave the man with the badge their full attention. Parker looked anything but pleased to see him.

'You're getting to be a regular nuisance, Brown. What do you want with me this time?'

Mark Brown dismounted slowly, making quite sure that his hands were clearly in view all the time and that nobody could think that he was about to draw. Most of the dozen or so men in the clearing were also carrying pistols at their hips and he did not wish to precipitate a needless gun fight. Once he was on the ground, he strolled over to the half-completed log cabin and eyed it with disapproval.

'Well,' said Parker, 'I asked you what you wanted with me today?'

'Last time I was here, Mr Parker, I asked you to make sure that your boys didn't trouble folk living either in town or out on their farms. Maybe you didn't think you needed to listen to my advice?'

Randolph Parker was staring at the star on Brown's jacket. He said, 'What game is this? You're no sheriff.'

'You're wrong about that, Mr Parker. I've been sworn in as a peace officer and I'm here to tell you that you had best call off your bullies.'

'Bullies, is it?' said the other man, his face growing red with anger. 'You think you can come on to my land and talk so?'

'I reckon,' said Brown laconically. He walked closer to the cabin and said, 'You wouldn't be fixing for to set this thing down somewhere and claim a hundred and sixty acres? It's illegal. You know that as well as I do.'

The sheriff strolled round the crude structure, examining it from various angles. Parker stood nearby, simmering.

While the other men stood still, wondering whether they were supposed to carry on working, there was a thunder of hoofs and five men galloped up. They looked, to Brown's eyes, like the sort of irregular forces that he had encountered during the war. He was put in mind of a group of Quantrill's raiders that his unit had once brought to heel.

The riders were all dressed in semi-military style, with boots which wouldn't have been out of place on a troop of cavalry. They all had military style scabbards at the front of their saddles which held carbines, and all but one carried two pistols. All in all, they were a pretty formidable-looking party. One of them said to Parker. 'Heard you might need a little help, Cap'n.' He turned a cold eye on Mark Brown, saying, 'This here the teacher I hear so much about?'

'I'm the teacher, but I combine that job with another. You might not have heard, but I'm now the sheriff for this district.'

'You say what?' exclaimed the man in amazement. He looked across to Parker and said, 'That right? There's a sheriff here, now? And this is him?' The man's tone was slightly truculent and aggrieved, as though here was a new factor which he had not previously needed to take into account.

Parker shrugged. 'It don't signify,' was all that he said.

In a leisurely and unhurried way, Mark Brown finished his inspection of the log cabin and when he had done so, he mounted his horse. He looked across the glade at Randolph Parker and said, 'You be sure and recollect what I have told you, Mr Parker. Remember these two points. First off is where I don't want to hear of anybody else being driven off their own land. I wouldn't even think about loading this heap of junk on to the back of a cart, and then plonking it down and claiming that it's a homestead. Second, I don't want to see your boys in town for a few days. If they want to come in for provisions, they aren't to be carrying weapons. Is that clear?'

What was clear was that Parker didn't take at all to being spoken to like that in front of his men. He was purple with rage. Apparently not noticing this, Brown tipped his hat and then turned his horse to ride off. As he did so, the five men on horseback moved into a line to block his path. Brown reined in his horse and said quietly, 'What will you men have?'

The tension grew for a second or two and several of the men who had been sawing logs, hurried to get out of what they conceived to be the line of fire. Then Randolph Parker said, 'Ah, let the bastard go.' The other riders moved a few inches to one side and Brown rode on. His legs almost brushed against those of the other men as he passed by.

As he rode away, the new sheriff felt an uncomfortable tickling between his shoulder blades, which he took to mean that he was being watched. He half-wondered if he would be shot in the back, but nothing happened. 'That was a close one, boy!' he muttered to himself.

Brown was two miles further down the road, clear of Parker's place and congratulating himself on his narrow escape, when the shooting began. The first shot went past his ear so close, he could hear it buzzing like a hornet. He spurred on his horse so the next one was a little wider. He was in a little ravine, with steep and wooded slopes rising on either side. The shots had come from the right and since there had not been another, after those first two, he supposed that he was now out of view of the man.

Slipping off his horse and drawing his pistol, Brown headed straight up the slope, darting silently from tree to tree, trying not to give anybody the chance to draw down on him. When he'd climbed a fair way up, he began to move back along the slope, in the direction from which he had come. All the while, he was looking down towards the track, scanning the trees for any movement or glimpse of colour which was out of the ordinary. Then he saw it. A flash of red. He froze behind the trunk of a pine tree; cocking the Navy Colt with his thumb, he waited and watched.

The man who came scrambling up towards him was dressed like the riders who had turned up while he had been talking to Parker. Same military-looking boots, patrol jacket and two six-shooters. This man was also carrying a rifle, a Winchester by the look of it. It had been the bright red neckerchief which had given him away and enabled Brown to spot him through the trees. For a bet, this was another of Parker's Texans and had probably been dispatched here to take him out as he passed by. They couldn't have known then that he was now a sheriff, and it had probably just been done on the assumption that he was a busybody who would be better under the ground than walking over it and causing trouble.

The fellow would pass no more than ten or fifteen feet from Brown, so he just waited patiently. Did the man think that he had killed him? Maybe he'd just been told to deliver a warning. When the other man was level with him and before he himself had been spotted, the teacher said, 'Just set that rifle down on the ground, now.'

The man whirled round, cocked his piece and began to raise it to fire. Shooting him down was a reflex action for Brown and his ball took the other in the middle of his chest. He dropped the rifle and sank slowly to his knees, an expression of disbelief on his face. There's a man who never expected to meet another fellow who was quicker or more ruthless than he was, thought Brown to himself. He went over and kicked the rifle to one side. 'You would o' done better to have dropped your gun when I first told you,' he informed the man, whose only response was to topple sideways into the carpet of brown pine needles. When he knelt down to check, Brown found that the gunman was already dead.

There seemed little more to be done there so Brown stood up and made his way back down the slope to where he had left his horse. Would the other men of his party figure out who had killed their partner? Almost certainly, he thought to himself. There'll be a reckoning for this, but then again trouble is coming my way already, if I'm not mistook.

The ride back to Barker's Crossing was uneventful and he got back to the livery stable by the time twilight was painting the fields a delicate shade of grey. Old Jack Brady who ran the stable was shutting up shop and looked a mite irritated to have a customer turn up right then. 'Come on, come on,' he said. 'Some of us have homes to go to. I can't be fooling round here all the night long.'

'I am paying you for this service,' Brown reminded him politely.

'That right that you're our sheriff now?'

'Yes. Where'd you hear it?'

'Jemima Clayton told me. Why, was you hopin' to keep it a secret?'

'Seems to me as that lady acts as a clearing-house for all the gossip in the neighbourhood,' said Brown, not best pleased to have his business being broadcast around the town.

The old man said, 'Oh, she ain't told everybody. She mentioned it to me on account o' we're kin.'

'Is there anybody in this town not related to Miss Clayton?'

'Oh she's only a second cousin of my mother's. It ain't a close connection. They're sayin' as you'll be needin' deputies soon. Call on me if you've need. I'd like to run some o' them scoundrels out of the town.'

'I'll bear the offer in mind. Thank you.'

Brady was standing a few feet from the sheriff and suddenly wrinkled up his nose and sniffed delicately. He leaned closer and said, 'Is that powder I can smell on you? You been shooting?'

'You needn't trouble about that,' said Brown hastily, 'There was something of a misunderstanding back on the road.'

The old man looked searchingly into his face and then said, 'Like I say, you want any help, I'm your man.

I'm what you might term a dab-hand with a scatter-gun.'

'Thanks,' said Brown, 'I'll surely remember that.'

At that moment, the old man grimaced in pain and looked as though he might be about to collapse. 'You all right?' asked the teacher. 'Here, why don't you sit down?'

'It's nothing, don't fuss,' said Brady testily. He turned towards the office, saying once again, 'Just remember me, if you want somebody who can shoot.'

Along Main Street, Brown passed several of his pupils, heading homewards with their mothers. The teacher sensed a certain reserve on the part of the mothers. It was nothing that he could put his finger on, just that they were not quite so easy with him as before. It wasn't until he had left them behind, that it dawned on him that he was now openly armed and wearing a star. They must wonder what the deuce is going on, he thought to himself. I'd best get this whole affair sorted out as soon as possible, so that I can stow this pistol back in my trunk and get back to teaching their children. It stands to reason that nobody cares for the sight of a schoolmaster who's marching round with a gun at his hip!

Miss Clayton appeared pleased to see her lodger. She said, 'I'm serving up some poached eggs, directly. I hope you're setting down at the table now and not gadding off somewhere else?'

'For somebody who was so mad keen on seeing me pick up a gun again, you can hardly complain now if being sheriff is keeping my time occupied,' replied Brown, smiling to show that he was just bandying words with the old woman playfully. 'A dish of poached eggs sounds just the thing right now. Thank you.'

When they were seated together and tucking in to the meal, Brown said, 'That fellow at the livery stable, Mr Brady, he says he's kin to you. That right?'

'In a roundabout way, yes, that's true.'

'It's a foolish question, but do you know if he really is any good with a shotgun? I mean a scattergun, those that you use for shooting game.'

'Why yes, he was famous for his ability to bring down birds in his younger days. He still goes out hunting. Sells game to people round here. If you're looking for somebody to guard your back, you could do a heap worse than Jack Brady.'

The teacher laughed. 'It seems to me, ma'am, that if you had your way I'd be operating with a whole posse of your friends and relations.'

'You given any more thought to my nephew in that respect?'

'Ma'am, you are incorrigible,' said Mark Brown, laughing out loud, 'So I promise you that if I ever feel the need for any deputies, then I'll keep your various cousins and nephews in mind.'

Brown recollected this conversation two days later, when he started hunting in earnest for men who would assist him in his duties as sheriff.

*

The following day was as quiet and peaceful as you could hope. Brown taught his children and not one of Parker's men showed up in town. It was beginning to look as though his straight-talking had worked some effect upon the rancher. It was surprising that nobody had come looking for him in connection with the man he had shot, but there it was. Perhaps there would be no further bloodshed and reason would prevail.

That Tuesday evening, Brown took a turn around the town and observed that the whole of Barker's Crossing was quiet. It was most agreeable, and he was getting ready to congratulate himself on the skilful way that he had dealt with what could easily have blown up into a very ugly situation.

When he went to bed that night, Mark Brown was feeling pretty pleased with himself. He had stopped Randolph Parker dead in his tracks and warned him away from the town. True, he had killed a man in the process, but nobody could deny that this had been self-defence. All in all, he had handled things well enough. Then, as he was saying his prayers before getting into bed, he recollected what the Scripture says about pride leading to destruction and so on. He tried to put himself in a slightly more humble frame of mind before drifting off to sleep.

CHAPTER 6

It seemed to Mark Brown that he had no sooner rested his head on the pillow that night, than that there was a knocking at his door, with somebody urging him to rise. He looked round and saw that it was pitch dark. Was the house on fire or something? Why would anybody want him to get out of bed in the middle of the night? As he came to, he recognized Miss Clayton's voice. She sounded scared.

'Mr Brown, do get up. There's need of your services.'

'Give me a chance to get dressed, ma'am,' he called out groggily. 'I'll be there directly.'

'Do hurry.'

As he pulled on his trousers and fastened his shirt, Brown tried to figure out what kind of crisis might be demanding his urgent attention at this ungodly hour. It could hardly be school business, which, by a natural process of elimination, left his role of sheriff as the reason that he was being roused at. He struck a

Lucifer and consulted the pocket watch at his bedside; ten past two in the morning.

When he felt that he looked reasonably decent and presentable, Brown emerged from his room, to find the old woman standing on the landing, with a lamp in her hand. 'What's the commotion all about?' he asked. 'I hope it's important.'

'It's important,' she answered grimly, 'There's a visitor downstairs for you.'

'For me? At this time of night? Who is it?'

'You'd best come down and see.'

Waiting in the parlour were two people. One was a woman that Brown had seen about town now and then, but whose name he did not know. The other was Patrick McDermott. He was wearing only a nightshirt and his bare feet were streaked with blood. 'Patrick,' he said, 'What ails you, son? What's amiss?'

'It's my ma, sir.'

'Your mother, you say? What of her?'

'She's . . . she's . . . she's . . . dead!' And at that fatal word, 'dead', the boy commenced weeping and sobbing like a little child. Instinctively, Brown went over to him and put his arms around the distressed boy. Patrick buried his face in the man's shoulder and cried his heart out. While this was going on, the teacher looked up at the two women and asked in a low voice:

'Anybody know what this is about?' Miss Clayton and the other woman shook their heads. He said, 'How does the boy come to be here?'

'I was lying in bed and heard a wailing and weeping. When I looked from my window, this young fellow was wandering about in the road outside. He was plumb distracted and so my husband said as I should get dressed and fetch him here to you.'

'I'm sorry,' said Brown, 'But I don't recollect your name?'

'I'm Mary Proctor.'

'Well, it's right good of you to bring Patrick here, Mrs Proctor. Was he wearing shoes when you found him?'

'No, sir. Looks to me like he walked barefoot all the way here. No wonder his feet is cut to ribbons.'

It was true; the boy had left bloody footprints across the carpet. Brown said, 'Mrs Proctor, you have done your piece and we're grateful for it. Why don't you cut along back home now?'

'If you're sure there's nothing more I can do?'

'No, me and Miss Clayton will manage well enough. Thank you again.'

After Mary Proctor had left, the teacher tried to dismiss Miss Clayton to bed in the same way, but the old woman wouldn't hear of such a proposal. 'I think I know my duty better than that, Mr Brown,' she said stoutly. 'We'll want to bathe that poor child's feet before we go any further. I'll boil up some water.'

She was as good as her word, and it didn't take long for the two of them to clean and dress the cuts and lacerations which covered the soles of Patrick McDermott's feet. After that had been done, with the boy himself accepting their ministrations stoically, without speaking a word, Brown said, 'You won't be able to sleep this night until you've told your tale, son. You can sleep in my bed, with Miss Clayton's leave, and I'll do well enough on the settee here. That all right, ma'am?'

Old Miss Clayton waved the question away as though it were of no import. She said, 'Happen this boy will speak more easily if it's just you and him together. I'll bid you both goodnight.'

After the old woman had gone back upstairs, Brown said, 'Come on then, Patrick. You best get this off your chest and tell me what befell you this night.'

The calm and authoritative way that his teacher spoke acted on the boy as a sedative and with no sobbing or tears, he set out precisely what had chanced a few hours earlier.

'It was dark. Ma was readin' to me and talkin' 'bout what I'd been doing at school. Been dark for an hour or more, I guess. Then we hear horses, riders. Sounded like a fair bunch o' men and Ma went out to see what they wanted. There was maybe ten of 'em. Couple had rifles aimed at her, soon as she walk out the house. Some of the others was holding pine brands aloft, so that everything was lit up in the flames.'

'You recognize any of the men?' asked Brown. 'Ever see any of 'em before?'

'Yes, sir, one of them had come by the house with Mr Parker a few days back. I knew him all right.'

74

'What did they say, son?'

'They said as Ma had been stealin' cattle from the range. They said that she'd taken mavericks and given them her own brand. Ma laughed at them. She said, "What in the hell do I want with his cattle? I got enough o' my own to tend to." 'The man I seed before, he says, "My boss has had enough o' you people cuttin' him off from his water rights and now rustlin' into the bargain."'

'What did your ma say to that?'

' 'Fore he talk of rustling, Ma was kind of laughin' at them, like she didn't think it was any real trouble. When he say rustling though, I could tell that she was getting scared. She bent down to me and said, "Patrick, don't you make a fuss about it, but you kind o' shuffle away off into the shadows, you hear what I say?" I said to her, "Ma, I don't want to leave you." but she said, "Son, you got to get ready to run all the way to town if needs be. Do as I bid you."'

The boy was trembling and cold, so the teacher reached out and drew Patrick to him, putting his arm round his shoulders and saying, 'It's best you tell me the whole thing, son. Else you won't sleep this night. Go on.'

'I did like Ma had told me and kind of moved out of the way. They didn't set any notice to me, they only wanted Ma. Couple o' the men, they get down off they horses and go to the pen to look at our calves. They say, "This'uns one o' ours for a bet. She done stole it!" Then another man gets down and he says to Ma,

"Aggie, we're agoin' to take you to see Mr Parker, see what he makes o' this here." She said, "What are you talkin' of?" I could tell she was real scared now. Then two of them, they tied her hands behind her back.'

'What next?' said Brown, his own face ashen, guessing as he could the outcome of all this.

'Just then, more riders fetch up and they got Mr Avery with 'em. I guess they took him prisoner too, because he has his hands tied together in front, so's he could ride his horse, but not fight or nothing. He says to my ma, "Hallo Aggie, these scallywags been troubling you as well?" He kind of laughed when he said it, like he didn't think much of those men. He turns to them and says, "You're a brave set, I don't think. Untie my hands and I tell you now, not one of you cowards durst face me in a fair fight."

'They got Ma on to a horse as well and then the leader says, "We change our minds. We ain't agoin' to take you to Mr Parker at all. We'll show you how we deal with rustlers where we come from." You know that old tree outside our house?'

Brown nodded, sick at heart.

'They threw ropes over a branch and tied them to another branch. They must have planned it all before, sir, 'cause there were nooses already on the end o' them ropes. Mr Avery, he said, "Are you mad? You men'll answer for this." They didn't take not a morsel of notice. Just brought my ma and Mr Avery right to the tree and said, "You got any last words?" Mr Avery, he say, "Let the woman go. Hang me if you must, but let her be." The leader of those men, he just told his men to get on with it. They put those ropes round their necks and then somebody fired a gun a couple o' times and the horses bolt.'

'All right, son,' said the teacher, 'That's enough now. You came here barefoot, through the night? You're a brave one. Your mother would have been proud of you.'

'Ma set a store by you, sir,' said the boy. 'Any time I had a question, she'd say, "You ask that Mr Brown. He'll know." '

'Did she, though? I thought a lot of her too. And now, before I get you tucked up in bed for the night, I'm going to tell you something which might make you feel a tiny bit better.'

'What's that, sir?' asked Patrick listlessly, as though he couldn't conceive of anything that would improve his situation.

'I promise you now, boy, that those men who did that to your ma will answer for it. I'll hunt every last one of 'em down and make them pay. It's not much comfort, but it's all I can offer you right now.' He stood up. 'Let's get you to bed now. You've had the roughest night I ever heard tell of.'

Mark Brown didn't sleep too well after he had seen Patrick safely to his bed. For one thing, the settee was lumpy and uncomfortable, for another, his mind was racing and sleep was long in coming. He kept thinking about the cold-blooded murder of a woman. It was the foulest crime he had ever witnessed and he had come across a few bad cases in his work for the marshal's office.

It was not the first murder of a woman he had encountered, but the others had been carried out in hot blood; husbands bludgeoning their wives to death when they were in their cups or lovers' quarrels which had got out of hand. This present case had clearly been planned well in advance. It was monstrous.

Mark Brown had never been a hasty man, which perhaps accounted for his success as a peace officer. He was not a one to rush in, not without weighing up all the pros and cons carefully first. This business would need a good deal of thought. There would be little point in him charging up to Parker's ranch and being shot down for his troubles. He would have to take it step by step.

Mrs Clayton was up early. She was a tough and indomitable woman, but it was plain that the events of the previous night had left her shaken. Brown filled her in on the rough outline of what had become of Cattle Aggie. She started in shock when he told her that Linton Avery had also been the victim of this brutal crime and tears came to her eyes. He said, 'There's no occasion for you to be involved further in this affair, ma'am. I'll take young Patrick over to the schoolroom and I can put him up there.'

'I won't hear of such a thing,' she said, with a flash of asperity. 'The child stays right here, leastways 'til we know what's to be done with him.'

'That's real good of you,' said the teacher gently, 'But it might prove dangerous. That boy is the only witness who can bring the crime home to those who committed it. It might be that an effort will be made to silence him. I mean somebody might want to kill him.'

'Somebody would kill a child?'

'I don't want you to be put at hazard, ma'am.'

'Pah, I ain't afeared of those rascals. You go and do what's needful and leave the boy in my care. There's no point debating the matter further, Mr Brown. My mind is quite set on that subject. If nothing else, I reckon I owe it to my late brother-in-law.'

Before leaving the house, Brown tiptoed into the room to see how Patrick McDermott was doing. By a great mercy, the boy was sound asleep. Taking care not to disturb him, the teacher took his gun belt from where it hung at the foot of the bed. Then he carefully closed the door behind him, bid Miss Clayton farewell and headed into the centre of town.

CHAPTER 7

It was a bright, sunny spring morning. Everything looked fresh and new. Although it was only a few minutes after eight, there was plenty of activity in Barker's Crossing. On Main Street, the stores were raising their shutters, and even the saloon had its doors open to air the place of the fug which had built up the previous night.

The main thing on Brown's mind that morning was putting together a band of men who would go with him up to the Parker ranch and bring in those responsible for last night's lynching. Before that, though, he would need to ride out to Patrick's home and see if there was any evidence that would serve to connect Randolph Parker or his employees with last night's events.

Jack Brady was already up and about. He said, 'You'll be wanting your horse, I reckon. What's afoot this morning? Not teaching school?' In all the alarms and excursions of the last few hours, Brown was horrified to realize that he had completely forgotten about the school. After his mare was tacked up, he rode to the school and waited to turn away the pupils as they arrived. This took some time and a few of the children appeared to suspect that something untoward had happened. It was hard to keep anything secret in a little town. It wasn't until a quarter after nine that he was able to get off and ride to the McDermotts' home.

When he got there, the scene was every bit as ghastly as he had feared. During the course of his career, Mark Brown had seen the aftermaths of a few lynchings. They were always ugly and the men who suffered such deaths invariably died hard; choking and struggling as they kicked out their lives on the end of the rope. Never yet though had he seen a woman treated so.

The faces of both Aggie McDermott and Linton Avery were suffused with blood until they were a dark purple. Their eyes were open and bulging from the sockets. Brown forced himself to dismount and begin searching the ground around the hanging bodies carefully. There were plenty of hoof prints, but nothing to distinguish one from another. Other than that, there were a couple of burnt out pine torches. These, he examined carefully and then stowed in his saddle-bag. There was an outside chance that he might be able to match these up with some tree over at Parker's spread. It was a slender enough hope, though. There were plenty of pine trees in the area.

When he had satisfied himself that there were no clues to be found, Brown went into the soddie and found a sharp kitchen knife. This he used to cut down the bodies. They fell to the ground with a bump and he wished that there had been somebody there to ease them down and treat the corpses with some respect. It was hard to know what to do with the bodies. In the end, he decided to take them back to town. There was a light cart at the back of the soddie and he managed to harness his own horse up to this, after a fashion. Having done this, the teacher tried, in the most dignified way possible, to lay the mortal remains of Aggie McDermott and Linton Avery on the back of the wagon. He felt terrible about dumping them down on the dusty wooden surface like that, but it seemed better than to leave them hanging from the tree or lying there on the ground. Once the bodies were loaded up, he headed back to town.

The sight of two corpses with horribly contorted faces, both lying on the back of a farm cart, was not a common one in Barker's Crossing. Mark Brown was perfectly well aware of this and was by no means displeased at the attention which this awful sight attracted when he parked the cart right bang in the centre of Main Street. He didn't make a big production out of the business, just halted outside the Chivers' store and then waited. At first, those passing along the boardwalk could scarcely believe their eyes. One or two people paused to double check that they had really seen two dead bodies at the back of a wagon driven by the town's teacher. Within a quarter hour, something of a crowd had begun to develop, although a very small and constantly changing one. Brown himself said nothing. He just sat there on the buckboard, ready to answer questions and give his views and opinions about the matter.

'Is that Aggie McDermott?' asked one man.

'That it is,' Brown replied, offering no further information. He wanted to rouse these men and this seemed as good a way as any to stir their curiosity. He felt a little uneasy about making use of the bodies in this way, but then the end in this particular instance surely justified the means. He would need at least a dozen or more men if he was going to be challenging Randolph Parker's boys.

'What happened to them, Mr Brown?' asked another man.

'They was lynched by men working for Parker,' Brown replied baldly. 'A man and woman, murdered in cold blood.'

There were murmurs of disgust and disapproval. Nothing, though, which sounded like anger; merely a sense that those viewing the two at the back of the cart felt that this was all a bit much. He wanted stronger emotions than that and his heart began to sink. He had a dreadful feeling that the folk of Barker's Crossing were likely to dismiss this as some species of private quarrel between Randolph Parker and the homesteaders.

Parking the cart outside the store where Mr Chivers

had been shot, was a calculated move on Mark Brown's part. The window shattered by gunfire was still boarded up and he hoped that displaying the corpses here would serve to remind the townsfolk that they too were the victims of Parker's men. His strategy though, did not appear to be working. No large and angry crowd was gathering around him, ready to swear vengeance. What was happening was rather that men and women were drifting up, tutting with dismay at the sight of these two dead people and then wandering off again. There were a dozen people standing around the cart, but they only looked for a few minutes and then went off again, to be replaced by newcomers. There was disgust and pity aplenty, but not the kind of anger which would make them likely to join a posse.

Of course, even if the men stopping to view the mortal remains of Aggie McDermott and Linton Avery had been so inclined, that would not be the end of the story. The fact was, Brown had no idea how he would be able to pay them even a nominal sum for riding with him in pursuit of justice. The more he thought about it, the more it struck him that he should have settled this matter with Avery, while that worthy man was still in the land of the living. Brown didn't even know how he would get any money himself for his law-keeping activities, let alone pay a bunch of men ten dollars a head to ride with him in a raid on Parker's ranch. This was a regular conundrum, and what the answer could be, he had not the least notion.

Slowly, even the small and variable group that had been congregating round the cart, evaporated and Mark Brown was left sharing the farm wagon with two dead people. There didn't seem a whole lot of reason to hang about any longer and so he decided to see about getting a funeral arranged. He only hoped that the parson at the church wouldn't expect him to pay for the job.

The Reverend Phillips was more than a little taken aback to find that the teacher, whose ambitions to join the ranks of clergy he knew about and approved of, was now turning up outside his home with a couple of horrible-looking corpses loaded on the back of a cart.

'Mr Brown,' said the minister, when he answered the door, 'It surely is good to see you. Have you come to talk about your plans?'

'In a sense, sir,' said Mark Brown, 'But first there is a little matter which I need to clear up.' It was then that he explained to the Reverend Phillips about his cargo. As he spoke, Phillips noticed the inconspicuous badge on the teacher's jacket and realized that the afternoon was not going to be pleasantly spent, being godly and holy in a self-satisfied way; but would rather entail some unwelcome action from him. He listened to Brown's account of the recent tragedy, agreed that it was terrible and that something needed to be done.

At first, the minister had a dreadful fear that it was Mark Brown's intention to draft him into a posse. When he learned that it was only being asked of him that he read the burial service for the dead over the two graves, he was mightily relieved. He said, 'Only thing is, Mr Brown, the fellow that usually digs the graves for me isn't in town right now.'

'I'll dig the graves,' said the teacher at once. 'What can we do about coffins, though? We'll want to get these two in the ground as soon as may be.'

'We generally use winding sheets, rather than coffins,' explained the minister. 'There's not enough people living and dying round here to tempt anybody to set up trade as a coffin-maker. If you're going to dig the graves, then you might care to prepare the bodies too. There'd be no occasion to remove the clothes of course. Just wrap the winding sheet round each of them.'

The hard physical exertion of digging two graves served to focus Mark Brown's mind. It was obvious to him that the citizens of Barker's Crossing were hoping against hope that if they just kept quiet and ignored what was going on a few miles from their town, then the struggle between the rancher and the homesteaders would not affect them overmuch. Even old Mr Chivers's death had not shaken them in this belief, nor had the increasingly outrageous actions of Parker's men in demanding free drinks from the Luck of the Draw. They honestly thought that this would all blow over without harming their own interests. And to that end, they were prepared to see one woman driven from her own land and another murdered in cold blood.

One aspect of that scene today in Main Street had

struck Brown, and that was the lack of curiosity shown by the town's inhabitants about the details of Aggie McDermott's death. It was almost as though if they didn't enquire too closely, then they might be able to persuade themselves that this was not quite such a foul crime after all. This indicated to the teacher the path that he should take. Accordingly, when once he had finished preparing things for the funeral, he put his jacket back on and made his way to Miss Clayton's house.

Young Patrick was up and about. His eyes were red from weeping, but he seemed to have got over the worst of it. Miss Clayton had got him to read to her, which was evidently having a calming effect. 'Patrick,' said the teacher, 'I have been up to your farm. It was all as you said and I have made arrangements for the funerals of your mother and Mr Avery.' It seemed to Brown that there was no point pussyfooting around and that speaking plainly in this fashion might be better for the boy.

So it proved, because Patrick McDermott replied, in an almost adult tone of voice, 'That's right good o' you, sir.'

'If you've no objection, I intend for your ma to lie next to Linton Avery. I gather they were great friends?'

Incredibly, after such an ordeal, the boy smiled faintly at this delicate way of putting the case. He said, 'He was sweet on Ma, if that's what you mean, Mr Brown.'

'Good, that's that settled. The funeral will take

place tomorrow morning. I'll say a few words then, if you've no objection?'

'Thank you, sir. Ma always thought well of you.' The use of the past tense in referring to his mother was too much for the child, and his eyes began to fill with tears. Miss Clayton clucked sympathetically and went over to put her arms round the distressed boy.

Feeling it better to take no notice of Patrick's display of grief, for fear of embarrassing the boy, Brown addressed Miss Clayton. 'I have a job for you, ma'am, if you'd care to take it on. It touches upon obtaining justice for your brother-in-law and Patrick's late mother. I mind you know most everybody in this here town. I want you to spread the word far and wide that the funerals will be conducted tomorrow at eleven in the morning. You might venture to suggest as it would be fitting for as many people from the town to attend as possible.'

'You'll have a full house, don't you fret about that, Mr Brown,' said the old woman firmly. 'They'll be there if I got to drag 'em to the burying ground by the scruff of their necks. Anything else you want I should do?'

'I wonder if you might have such a thing as some paper and envelopes, ma'am?'

'You want to catch up with your correspondence? I'd have thought you had more pressing matters to concern you right now.'

Brown smiled. 'This has some bearing on the matter in hand,' he said. 'I'm not planning to write to my folks back home, describing the weather or telling them about the scenery here or anything of that sort.'

He didn't feel it necessary to mention the matter to Miss Clayton, but the teacher had already made some provisional plans for dealing with things if the rest of the town felt inclined to sit tight and hope that the trouble with Randolph Parker would blow over. He certainly hoped to deliver a moving eulogy on the morrow and stir up the folk in Barker's Crossing to such a pitch that they would join him in bringing justice to the dead woman and her friend; but the wise man does not place too much hope in the variable and constantly changing opinions of others. Brown already knew at least two or three people in town who might be of practical assistance to him in his endeavours and it was upon them that he intended to rely.

Pete Cartwright opened the door and did not appear to be at all surprised to see the teacher standing on the step. Indeed, he looked rather as though he had been expecting him. 'Oh, it's you, Mr Brown. Won't you come in?'

Cartwright's wife was also at home and she once more gave him fulsome and effusive thanks for rescuing their daughter from her difficulties. Fact was, with all that was going on, Brown had all but forgotten about that little episode. Once she had stopped talking, Pete Cartwright despatched her to the kitchen to make some coffee. He said, 'Take a turn around the garden with me, Mr Brown. We can talk easier in the fresh air.'

The Cartwrights' garden was scarcely bigger than their kitchen and Brown rightly gauged that he had been brought out here, not so much to admire the little patch of herbs growing by the back door, but rather so that Emma Cartwright couldn't hear what was being said.

'Like my wife said, we're in your debt for what you did the other night for Lily-May. Happen I misjudged, but you have the way about you of a man about to call in a debt.'

'I wouldn't put it so. I came to ask you a favour.'

Cartwright looked a little uncomfortable. True, he had, on the spur of the moment and in his relief at hearing about the fix from which his daughter had been rescued, promised to help the teacher if needed, but from all that he was able to apprehend, events were moving swiftly towards a bloody climax and he had a family to think of. He surely hoped that Brown wasn't going to ask him to volunteer as a deputy.

Something of what was going through the man's mind must have shown on his face, because Mark Brown said hastily, 'I ain't about to ask you to fight by my side, you needn't fret about that.'

'What then?'

'I want you to run an errand for me. It'll take two or three days, there and back. Can you do that?'

'I reckon. What is this errand?'

'You know the army base, away over east? It's called Fort Jackson and it's about twenty-five miles from here.'

'Sure I know it. Been by there a couple o' times. That where you want me to go? What for?'

'I want you to deliver this letter to the officer in charge of Fort Jackson. Nobody else, mind. Only the fellow in charge. Think you can do it?'

'Sure. Is that all? I was afeared you might have it in mind that I would ride down with you on those bandits and have a set-to with 'em.'

'You got young'uns to care for. I wouldn't ask such a thing of a family man.'

Brown produced a long, thin envelope from his jacket and handed it to Pete Cartwright. He said, 'This could mean life or death, not just to me, but others in this town. Ride hard.'

As soon as he had laid eyes on the hanging bodies of Cattle Aggie and Linton Avery, the teacher had known that things had gone far beyond what one man could deal with, however tough and resourceful that man might be. No, he needed help and urgently at that, if he was to be able to prevent the deaths of any more innocent people. As he rode back to Barker's Crossing, Brown's mind had worked furiously, trying to come up with a plan. By the time he had reached the outskirts of the town, he thought that he had at least the germ of an idea.

As a marshal, law had never been Mark Brown's strong suit. He was handy enough with his fists, could use most any firearm to be found and was utterly without nerves. His usual procedure was to bring in the man he was hunting and then leave it to others to decide on the finer points of the charges against him. Still and all, he had some knowledge of statutes, including the ones passed in the aftermath of the War Between the States.

The Enforcement Acts had provided for the use of Federal troops to come to the aid of the civil power. Although they were primarily designed to cope with problems in the defeated Confederate states of the south, they were applicable to the whole of the United States. A representative of the civil government could request military assistance against rebel forces, the Ku Klux Klan and so on. It was surely worth trying to call for the help of the army against these Southerners. It was a question of making the appeal look legal and urgent. After a lot of deliberation and much racking of his brains for the correct spelling of various words, the document which Brown had written in Miss Clayton's house and now required Pete Cartwright to deliver to the military at Fort Jackson read thus:

To Officer Commanding, Fort Jackson
April 15th, 1875

Sir,

I, Sheriff Mark Brown, am the only representative of the Civil Power in the town of Barker's Crossing, Wyoming Territory. A band of armed marauders, consisting of irregular forces of the former Confederate Army, have arrived in the neighbourhood and begun to commit various acts of warfare, including murder, mayhem, looting and rapine. Four individuals have been deprived of their civil rights by being hanged or shot to death.

One of the victims of these actions by Rebel Forces was Justice of the Peace Linton J. Avery. I am accordingly the only representative of the Civil Power in this part of the Territory of Wyoming. Under the powers vested in the Federal Army by the Enforcement Acts of 1870 and 1871, I call upon you to provide urgent aid and assistance to suppress this rebellion.

I have the honour to remain, Sir,

Your Obedient Servant, Mark Brown, (Sheriff).

When he had finished writing this appeal, Brown read it through and wondered whether or not he had laid it on too thick. Then he recollected himself and thought, well, it really is a matter of life and death. Not just my own life and death, either. If it gets the army to act, then I can argue the legality of the case afterwards.

Old Mr Brady looked pleased to see him when Brown fetched up at the livery stable. 'What's amiss? You looking to take your horse out or you want a deputy?' the old man asked shrewdly. 'That's a hell of a thing about Linton Avery and Aggie. Hell of a thing.'

'Miss Clayton tells me that you're quite the crackshot with a scattergun. That right?'

'I told you that already. What, you didn't take my

word for it?'

'Mr Brady,' said Brown wearily, 'If you'd been in law enforcement as long as me, you wouldn't take anybody's word for anything in the world. I tell you now, if my own brother told me that the sun was shining, I'd still look out the window to check. That's how you get when you work as a marshal or sheriff.'

'No offence meant or taken. Yeah, I reckon I'm the best shot with a scattergun for miles around.'

'You still in practice? You ain't gone rusty or aught?'

At this, Jack Brady burst out laughing. He said, 'You not heard o' my little sideline? When I ain't running this place, you'll like as not find me up in the hills, hunting. Birds, deer, jack-rabbits. You name it, I kill it and sell it to folk around here. You ask anybody, don't take my word for it.'

Mark Brown stared out across the rooftops of Barker's Crossing, gazing at the distant hills. Without turning his eyes to the owner of the livery stable, he said, 'You still want to be a deputy?'

'Wouldn't have offered, else.'

'Well then, like as not I'll swear you in tomorrow, straight after we bury Mrs McDermott and Linton Avery. I tell you straight though, things are apt to get damned hot. You sign up and you're putting your life at risk.'

'It's been a long one so far and I took a whole heap o' risks in it. You want a gun, then I'm your man. 'Side's which, Linton Avery was a good friend o' mine and kin to Jemima Clayton into the bargain. I'm your man.'

By good fortune, Brown didn't need to hunt out the next person he wished to see. Mrs Clayton's nephew Andy was sweeping the boardwalk in front of one of the little stores that fronted on to Main Street. He smiled and waved when he saw the teacher, crying, 'Hey there, sir! How's it doing?'

When he was a little closer to the boy, Brown said, 'You told me the other day as you wanted to be a deputy. You still game?'

'Why, I should just about say I am, sir,' said the youth, a broad, open and good-natured grin spreading across his face. 'Golly gosh, I reckon I can help you. Ain't nobody handles a rifle like me.'

There was something so artless and innocent about the boy, that Mark Brown felt a sudden misgiving, like he was fixing to take advantage of a child or something of that sort. He said, 'Listen here now, Andy. This is a serious business. You ride alongside of me, you could end up being shot. Killed even. You understand what I'm telling you?'

'I ain't a kid, Mr Brown. Course I understand and I'm tellin' you that I'll do it. I heard about Mr Avery. He was my great uncle twice removed or some such. Leastways, I know he was family to me and I ain't about to let his death go without doin' something about it. I'm in.'

'Good lad.'

It had been observed in the town that none of the hands from Parker's ranch had been in for a time and this had encouraged regulars to return to the Luck of the Draw. All in all, it felt like things were returning to normal and if the price of that normality turned out to be a couple of people who weren't really citizens of Barker's crossing at all, well then, so be it. This callous attitude was due to be rudely shaken the next day.

The morning of the funeral dawned with an overcast and leaden sky, heavy with the promise of rain to come. Patrick McDermott was still staying at Miss Clayton's and nothing Brown could say would persuade the old woman that her duty lay otherwise than in caring for a poor orphan child. She too, like the teacher, was very familiar with those passages in Scripture touching upon the care of widows and orphans.

True to her word, Miss Clayton had succeeded in rounding up an impressive congregation for Linton Avery and Aggie McDermott's burial service. There were so many mourners that the minister chose to hold the whole thing in the burying ground, rather than the church. It was, thought Brown, open to question how many of these folk had come because they wished to pay their respects to the dear departed and which of them had just turned up to see what might be said during the interment. Well, that was fine. He certainly had a few things to say, and the more of the inhabitants of Barker's Crossing who heard them, the better.

There was something distinctly lacking in dignity about the way that the wrapped corpses were placed in the open graves. With a coffin, you can make the whole process look very solemn and lower the casket gently into the grave. When you're handling a corpse in a winding sheet, the sight has a horrid fascination about it; it is so very plainly a dead body. It somehow looks far worse when you can see the shape of a head and feet when placing something like that in the ground.

First they sang a couple of hymns, starting with Amazing Grace and then said the Lord's Prayer. After that, the two bodies were somehow manoeuvred into their respective graves and the minister read the service for the dead. 'I am the resurrection and the life . . . whosoever believeth in me . . . in my father's house there are many mansions. . . .'

When the service was finished, everybody filed past and threw stones or handfuls of earth into the open graves. Then the minister asked if anybody would like to say a few words. As agreed, he looked directly at Mark Brown when he asked this question and the teacher stepped forward at once. He had given a great deal of thought about what to say. On the one hand, he didn't want to upset Patrick McDermott, who was doing his best to bear up manfully. On the other, though, he wanted to make his views quite clear and try to get these people raised to the right pitch of indignation.

'Friends,' he began, 'There's some of you known the departed for a lot longer than I have. I'm speaking now, though, in my position of sheriff, which some of you may know about. These two good folk were killed unlawfully. They didn't have a trial, they was just lynched. A woman lynched! I was a lawman for ten years and I tell you now, I never heard of such a thing before. Already, those as did this crime are causing trouble in this town. I see the owner of the Luck of the Draw over yonder, Mr Dowty. He knows what I'm talking about.' Brown paused for a second, observing the crowd narrowly to see how they were taking his address. It didn't look any too promising, because most of the people were shuffling and looking around uneasily. A few were glancing up to the sky, as though hoping that he would finish and be done with his speechifying before the rain started. He continued, 'I know that all you men, like me, would scorn to let such a crime as this go unpunished. I know who was involved in the murders and I'm riding out to bring them in, either today or tomorrow. I'm asking now, who will join me and be sworn in as deputies, just 'til this matter is settled?'

In truth, Brown hadn't expected a mad stampede of volunteers to ride to the Parker ranch. He had expected some, though. None of the men at the grave-side would meet his eye and those at the back were showing a tendency to slink away without anybody marking their departure. He said, 'Is there not one man here?' There was no answer and slowly, the crowd broke up and drifted away from the burying ground, leaving only Miss Clayton, Patrick McDermott, the minister and Brown himself. It began to rain and by the time that the three of them got back to Miss Clayton's house, it was pouring down in a veritable torrent.

CHAPTER 8

Not one of the men who attended the funeral that morning took at all to being berated by the town's teacher, never mind what post he now claimed to hold. His parting shot, asking if there were any men present, had been particularly poorly received. Although they didn't give voice to their feelings in the proximity of the church and so soon after a burial service at that, by the time they were back in their homes, not a few of the men gave their views and opinions of Mark Brown pretty freely to their families. Expressions such as 'cow's son' and 'bastard' were thrown around.

There was still no sign of Parker's men in the town, and so by evening, most of those who lived in Barker's Crossing were congratulating themselves on playing their hand right in keeping out of the lynchings affair. With a little luck, once Randolph Parker had asserted himself out in the wilds and reclaimed the open range for his herds, the town itself would return to normal and there would be no reason in the world for Parker to have a down on them. Quite a few of the men who had attended the funeral thought that some sort of celebration might be in order that evening, to mark the fact that the lightning had fallen elsewhere and that they themselves could now resume their ordinary lives. The Luck of the Draw was accordingly doing a brisk trade at about seven that evening when Mark Brown walked through the bat-wing doors and stood there, surveying the scene.

The rain hadn't let up all day and it was still lashing against the windows of the saloon. Brown himself was soaked to the skin and just stood there, dripping water on to the floor. At first, nobody noticed the slight figure by the door and the patrons of the Luck of the Draw just carried on drinking, talking and laughing. But little by little, men spotted the town's erstwhile teacher and nudged their companions; indicating with a nod of the head and roll of their eyes, the black-clad man standing and watching them. As others became aware of the sober man with his eyes upon them, so conversation dried up and laughter ceased, until there was dead silence. And still, Mark Brown just stood there, without saying a word. Then he spoke, his sharp, clear voice carrying across the whole of the bar-room.

'You're a set of cowards! Every man-Jack o' you drinking here right now. There's only two in this town as I would call real men who aren't afraid to set-to for what's right. One of them is a boy and the other an old man. As for the rest of you. . . .' He shook his head in disgust. 'You think you've bought your safety by turning a blind eye to the murder of a woman. You're wrong. All you done is abandon your honour.' Having delivered himself of this statement, Brown turned on his heels and left the saloon.

The rain was still falling and the sun just dipping below the horizon. With all the dark clouds above the town, twilight was falling early. In the distance, Mark Brown could see purple tongues of lightning licking at the hilltops which ringed Barker's Crossing. He stood there in the rain for a moment and then something caught his attention. It was the rumble of hoofs. A body of riders was approaching the town from the west. He might be wrong, but his cat's sense told him that these were Parker's men, coming to pay a visit.

There was no percentage in going up against an unknown number of skilled gunmen single-handed, not unless he was left with no other choice. Brown sprinted down Main Street towards the livery stable. Now it was time to see how much the promises of Jack Brady and Miss Clayton's nephew, Andy, were worth when it came down to it.

Old Mr Brady was sitting in his office with his feet up. In the dim yellow glow of the oil lamp, the teacher could see that Brady was reading a cheap Tauchnitz edition of some novel. 'Well,' he said, when Brown approached, 'Time for me to make good on my offer, is that the way of it?'

'Pretty much, Mr Brady. You still game for this?'

'You betcher,' said the old man. 'You want that I should bring my scattergun with me now?'

'If you got it here, then yes. That'd be a right good scheme.'

While Brady was reaching for his gun out of a closet and loading it, the teacher said, 'You know where Andy lives? Meaning Miss Clayton's nephew.'

'Andy Porter? Sure, he lives down the way a space. You want that we should go fetch him now?'

'Might be best.'

'You goin' to tell me what's afoot?'

'You weren't at the funeral this morning?'

'Some of us got work to do.'

Mark Brown sketched briefly the events of the day, bringing his narrative up to date by telling of the party of riders he had heard coming into Barker's Crossing. The old man took a small green bottle from a drawer of the desk, uncorked it and took a swig.

'Surely you ain't getting liquored up?' asked the teacher, slightly appalled.

'Liquor, nothing! This is medicine.'

'You're sick? What ails you?'

'That don't signify. You want we should stay here jawing or you want the use o' my gun?'

Brady closed up his office and, with his shotgun tucked under his arm, led the teacher down an alleyway to a little row of houses behind the stores on Main Street.

The rain was easing off a little, although there was still enough to make them both dripping wet by the time they knocked on the door of a neat little cottage, which was surrounded by a clipped hedge. A middle-aged woman opened the door and stared in alarm at the gun that Jack Brady was carrying. 'Heavens above, Mr Brady, what are you about? Can I help you?' She noticed Brown and greeted him as well, with a little more reserve.

'Good evening, Mrs Porter,' said the teacher, 'Is your son in?'

'Andy? What do you want with him?'

At that moment, the youth himself appeared in the doorway behind his mother. 'Hey, Mr Brown. Mr Brady.'

'Andy, if you really want to help me, then right now is your chance,' Brown told him. 'You want to be sworn in as a deputy, then fetch your rifle and come with us.'

Mrs Porter looked as if she was fit to die when she heard mention of her son's rifle. She exclaimed, 'Lord a mercy, what's going on?'

'Your son's asked if he can help me, me being sheriff and all, which you might not have known.'

'I never heard such foolishness,' declared Andy Porter's mother. 'You just get back into the parlour, Andy, you're going nowhere at all.' She addressed Brown angrily. 'You should be ashamed of yourself, a man your age trying to lure a boy into danger. You ought to know better as well, Mr Brady. Old gentleman like you.'

Andy had not argued with his mother, but

retreated back inside the house. Mark Brown had more or less written him off, when the youth appeared again behind his mother. This time, he was wearing an overcoat and hat and carrying a rifle. He said to his mother, 'I'm a-goin' out, Ma. Don't be afeared, I'll take care of myself. I told you before, I can't be sweeping floors all my life long. Lawkeeping's something I got a hankering after, you know that.'

When Randolph Parker had sent word to contacts of his in Texas, that he was looking for some lively boys who would undertake a little rough work, money no object, he didn't really know what he was letting himself in for. Some of the men already working for his outfit were pretty dangerous types; men who might knife a stranger over some fancied slight. The twenty-five men who came north into the Wyoming Territory that spring were something else again.

After the surrender at Appomattox Court House in 1865, there were quite a number of diehards in the South who did not feel inclined to end their war just then. Some of them proceeded to knock over banks, hold up trains and ambush Yankee army patrols for several months after the War Between the States had officially ended. When things grew too hot for them in Texas and New Mexico and the full rigours of reconstruction began to bite, some of these men crossed the border into Mexico and offered their services to Benito Juarez, who was at that time struggling to wrest control of his nation from the Emperor, whom the French had installed. By the time the war in Mexico had ended, there were a few hard-bitten souls who had been fighting in one war or another for the better part of ten years. Killing and looting was the only life some of them knew or could imagine.

A band of men from Texas and Georgia, who had been on Juarez's side, crossed back over the Rio Grande in 1873 and then made a perfect nuisance of themselves by teaming up with Comancheros and getting involved in all sorts of activities, from running guns to the Kiowa and Comanche to undertaking run-of-the-mill road agent work. Things were getting a little hot for this group of freebooters, when they received news that some rancher up in the north, well away from their usual area of action, wanted a bunch of men to go and throw some dirt farmers off his land.

What Parker didn't altogether understand was that these men were not really under his control at all, when once they had descended upon his ranch. Sure, they would kill a few men or women and help drive the settlers back to where they had come from; that was what they were being paid for. But having found that the nearest town to the ranch had no lawman and was full of men who seemingly had no appetite to stand up to them, the hired guns quite naturally turned their attention to Barker's Crossing. There were sure to be pickings of some sort to be had in such a town, even if it was only free drinks, the chance of a woman and whatever the stores there had, which could be made off with. They had stripped other little towns bare like a horde of locusts and there did not appear to be any good reason why they should not perform the same trick up here in the north.

The three men walked up Main Street towards the Luck of the Draw. When they were still a way from it, they saw, coming towards them, one of those whom Mark Brown recognized at once as being one of the southerners hired by Parker. 'Hold up now,' he said softly to his companions, 'I want to speak to this fellow.'

When the man was level with them and about to walk past, Brown said in a friendly enough way, 'Hey there, friend. Might I be having a word or two with you?'

'Yeah,' said the other, suspiciously. 'What's the problem?'

The teacher walked up to the man, smiling pleasantly, and said, 'There's no problem. It's only this. I'm sheriff in these parts and I am making sure that only residents of this town bear arms. I'll thank you to hand over that pistol I see at your hip.'

'My pistol? What in the hell are you talkin' about?'

'There's no call for strong language or blaspheming,' said Brown, no longer smiling, 'I'm telling you straight, hand me that gun.'

It was slowly dawning on the fellow that this was no game. The two men on either side of the sheriff had, without making any great show of it, moved away a few paces and were now holding their weapons as though ready and willing to bring them up to bear upon him. The men in this town might in general be walkovers, but even so, here were three men who were not to be blustered or bluffed into backing off. The man glanced up the street towards the saloon, hoping that some of his friends would appear, but there was nobody else about. Mark Brown said, 'Time's up, fella. Reach out that pistol, slow as you like.'

Stuart Singer had been in tighter spots than this present one. His hand snaked down towards the pistol, but he was not quite quick enough. The man standing before him, drew his own piece and then pistol whipped Singer round the side of the head. He put his full strength into the initial blow and then followed it up with a couple more cracks across Singer's face and then down on to the top of his head. As he fell stunned to the ground, the sheriff reached down and plucked the pistol from his grasp. Then, when Singer was kneeling there, holding his head and becoming aware of the blood trickling between his fingers, he received a sharp kick in the ribs which sent him sprawling. Brown finished off by stamping down hard on the outstretched arm of the man he had knocked down. There was a clear audible crack, like the snapping of a dry stick, as some bone in his arm fractured.

Jack Brady and Andy Porter watched this savage beating in shocked silence. It was the suddenness of the attack which had left them speechless with amazement. Most fights build up with a trading of insults and then proceed to tentative blows before heating up and getting serious. This was in a different league entirely. One second, the two men had been standing there, talking quietly and the next, one of them was laying in the dirt, nursing a broken arm and probably a case of concussion.

The teacher turned to his two deputies and said, 'That's one of those villains who'll not be wielding a gun today. I didn't smash up his wrist from cruelty. I don't want him firing on us at all. The odds are stacked high enough against us as it is.'

The change in Mark Brown was astonishing. Both Brady and Porter had been used over the last month to seeing this shy and reserved-looking man ignoring any number of sly jokes and contemptuous remarks directed against him. You would have thought that he was the meekest man alive. The sight of him exploding into violence in this way was a disturbing one. Brown must have picked up something of this from their demeanour, for he said, 'You needn't look at me like that. These are the men who killed a defenceless woman. They need to be taught a lesson and I'm the man to do it.' Then he paused for a second and a grim smile appeared briefly on his lips. 'After all, I'm the teacher, ain't I?'

Leaning down to where his victim was still stretched out, groaning in the dust of the road, Brown said to him, 'Why don't you tell your friends I'm out here and would be glad if they'd favour me with a few words? Tell 'em I'll be over yonder at the end of the street.'

'You bastard. You broke my arm.'

'You remember what I said to you about cursing

and such? If'n you don't want the other arm broke, then get yourself down to the saloon and do as I bid you.'

The injured man got slowly and painfully to his feet and walked towards the Luck of the Draw. Mark Brown turned to his two companions and said, 'Well, you boys with me or not? If you've no stomach for shooting and killing, now's the time to say.'

'I killed men before,' said old Jack Brady quietly, 'I reckon this lot deserve it.'

Andy Porter, being the youngest of them all, was still of an age to find fighting an exciting diversion. The beating of Parker's hired gun had thrilled him and he looked like he was ready for anything. He said, 'Hell, yeah. I'm with you, sir.'

'Not so much of the cursing,' said Brown reprovingly. 'Come on then, let's get ourselves into position.'

Singer's entrance to the saloon, minus his gun and with a busted arm, caused some little stir. He staggered through the doors and shouted out for his friends. There was the usual lively hubbub in the place, the saloon being crowded that night. There was a space around the bar though, where four of the men Randolph Parker had hired were drinking. They were armed to the teeth and had given the impression to the regular patrons of the saloon that they were in town for some specific purpose. This was quite true. Earlier that day, they had finally stumbled across the body of Quentin Haines, one of their number who had been missing for a few days. They had become increasingly uneasy at his absence, he not being the sort of man to run off and vanish without a word. He and his horse had apparently just disappeared into thin air.

It had been Stuart Singer and another man who had gone off to look for any sign of Haines. They knew that he had gone off to put a scare on the town's teacher, a black-clad milksop who looked liked a priest and had been asking a sight too many questions for anybody's liking. That had been the last anybody saw of their partner. Singer had suggested that it might be worth looking about in the pine woods lining the road from Parker's ranch to Barker's Crossing. It had been a cloud of buzzing flies which had first caught Singer's eye as they combed the area, and these turned out to be feasting upon the decomposed corpse of a man who had fought side by side with Singer through two wars.

By the time that five of Haines's old compatriots rode into town that evening, they had a pretty good idea that the one-time teacher, now evidently the sheriff in these parts, had been responsible for the death of their friend. There was a score to settle there. They had gone first to the saloon, to see if anybody knew where this precious teacher was to be found, but nobody seemed to know. Well, they could spare the time for a glass or two of whiskey, before they killed him.

Two of his friends assisted Stuart Singer to the bar, where he was given a stiff shot of rye. 'What happened, man?' asked somebody.

'It was that bastard teacher,' said Singer. 'He buf-faloed me, took me by surprise. I didn't even have a chance to draw. Then when he'd knocked me down, he used his boots and broke my damned arm.'

There was dead silence now in the saloon. Both the townsfolk and those working for Randolph Parker were listening intently to Singer's words. He said, 'The whore's son told me he'd be waiting for you boys down the road a-ways.'

'Left or right after we leave here?'

'Right.'

'You stay here, Stu. We'll settle him now and be back before you've finished that drink.' With a jin-gling of spurs and the click of heavy boots, the four men moved off from the bar and headed for the door. No sooner were they through the bat-wing doors, than there was a stampede, as all the other customers in the Luck of the Draw rushed out into the street to see what would follow.

Mark Brown had taken his stand right outside the corn chandler's, outside which was parked a buck-board. He was standing alongside this, in plain view when the four men from the south came looking for him. He felt relaxed and easy, maybe for the first time since he had fetched up in Barker's Crossing. Ever since he had quit being a marshal, Brown had been keeping himself under a tight rein. Now he was loose again and free to act as he pleased. It wouldn't do in the long run, not if he really was going to train for the ministry, but by Godfrey, there was something exhilarating about being able to deal with matters just as he pleased!

The four men from the saloon fanned out and stopped no more than thirty feet away. They had that swaggering air about them of men who do not have the slightest doubt that they are holding the winning cards. The teacher had guessed correctly that these fellows had taken counsel together and decided to kill him this night. Still and all, he had to give them the chance to back off, if they would listen to reason.

'Well, boys,' said Brown, 'What will you have? I aim to disarm the four of you. We can do it easy or we can do it hard. Which do you prefer?'

All four of the men standing there in front of him burst out laughing. They weren't putting on a show; this really was the funniest thing that they'd heard in a good, long spell. When they had recovered themselves, one of the men said, in an accent which was pure Georgian, 'Well now, I reckon we'll take it the hard way.'

Although he didn't know it, a man was already drawing down on the Georgian and preparing to fire. Deep in the shadows along the boardwalk, where the light of the moon was prevented from shining by the awnings above the storefronts, Jack Brady was crouching behind a barrel, his scattergun trained on the man who was bandying words with Mark Brown. Brady had taken first pull on the trigger and, in accordance with the teacher's instructions, he was waiting only for the Southerners to fire the first shot, before he himself joined in the fighting.

Laying on the roof of the smithy, on the other side of the street, Andy Porter was also getting ready to open fire. His heart was pounding and his mouth full of a strange coppery taste, like he might have been sucking pennies. It was the taste of fear, although mingled with the greatest excitement the boy had ever known. He had only ever shot squirrels, deer and birds, but that didn't mean he had never wondered what it would feel like to kill a man with his rifle. He squinted down the barrel, cocked his piece and waited for the shooting to start in the street below. Mr Brown had been most forceful in impressing upon Andy that he wasn't to shoot until if and when he saw the men who would be coming to find the teacher open fire. Once that happened, he could shoot away at them like they were jack-rabbits.

'You want it the hard way?' asked Brown sadly. 'Then I guess you boys had best pull your pistols, but recollect that I gave you the chance to settle this peacefully.'

All four of the men chuckled at these words, which sounded to them like the bravado of a man whistling in the dark. Then they went for their guns. As soon as he saw that first twitch of movement, Mark Brown dived for cover, throwing himself behind the nearby buckboard. The first bullets went wild as a consequence of this unexpected action on his part. The crack of pistol fire was answered almost immediately by the boom of a shotgun and then the sharper sound of rifle fire. He drew his own pistol, cocking it with his thumb as he did so and risked a quick glance round the side of the cart. Two of the men were down and the two others were turned away from him, trying to identify the source of the withering crossfire in which they were caught. Brown shot one of the men down and then the other fell; whether dropped by Andy's rifle or the old man's scattergun, he could not tell. He stood up and walked cautiously over to the four prone figures, shouting as he did so, 'You men hold your fire now!'

CHAPTER 9

The crowd of men from the saloon had all thrown themselves to the ground or dived back into the Luck of the Draw when the shooting started. As soon as it seemed to have ended, they picked themselves up, dusted themselves down and wandered casually over in the direction of the corn chandler's to see what had happened. Most had expected to see their new sheriff laying face down in the dirt and it came as no little surprise to find that he was moodily surveying the aftermath of the gun battle.

'Lord a-mighty,' said one awestruck individual, 'You kill all four of 'em yourself, Mr Brown?'

'No, I had some help.'

At that moment, young Andy came running up, eager to examine his handiwork. Jack Brady came over more slowly. He had killed men before and the novelty of the experience had long ago worn off. He wasn't particularly proud of shooting a man, and it was only his deep-rooted conviction that it had been right to revenge the needless death of a woman which had persuaded him to participate in such a bloodbath. Mark Brown noticed the sober expression on the old man's face and said quietly, 'I know how you feel, Mr Brady. It's the deuce of a thing to take a fellow being's life in this way.'

Brady shrugged and said, 'It ain't pleasant, but it's needful. You get a mad dog running round, the only thing to do is shoot it.'

Miss Clayton's nephew put the teacher in mind of a puppy who wishes to be praised. The youth said, 'Did I do all right, sir? I waited 'til they fired, just like you said.'

'You did just fine, Andy. I couldn't have wished for a better man to have up on that rooftop.'

On hearing himself described as a man, Andy Porter visibly swelled and threw out his chest like a bantam cock strutting around the farmyard.

All four of the men from Parker's ranch had died swiftly, which was another mercy. There are few things worse than dealing with a man who has had his belly blown open by a shotgun blast and trying not to let him see by any word or look that you know him to be doomed. Much better to die cleanly and immediately by a bullet through the head or heart; the fate which had befallen all these men.

One of the men from the saloon said, 'What happens next? I reckon Randolph Parker's going to be mighty vexed about this.'

Brown turned a cold eye upon the speaker. 'You

reckon that, do you?' he asked. 'You want to help me do anything about it?'

The man mumbled and if it had not been pitch dark, the others would have seen him flush a deep red. He said nothing more.

'What became of the other fellow?' asked Brown, 'Him as I ran into earlier?'

'Man with the broken arm? He came by the saloon just a few minutes back. It was on account of him that these rascals come looking for you. He said you'd be waiting for them.'

At that precise instant, Stuart Singer, the man whose arm Brown had broken, joined the group standing around the bodies of his former friends. He was holding his injured arm carefully, cradling it with his left hand like a makeshift sling. When he saw the four bodies, he looked as though he felt like swooning dead away in the street. He swayed unsteadily and a man standing next to him reached out a hand and placed it comfortingly on his shoulder. Singer shook it off angrily. He walked closer to the corpses and peered at their faces. These were all men who were closer to him than brothers; fellows that he had fought alongside, travelled with, drank with, gone whoring with and lived with for years. Now their lives had been snuffed out. He looked around for Mark Brown and when he saw him, he walked up to him and said, 'Don't you think this is over. It'll be blood for blood, you hear what I tell you now?'

'How well d'you shoot with your left hand?' said the teacher.

'Don't you bother 'bout which hand I shoot with,' said Singer. 'There's another twenty-odd men back at the ranch as'll take care of you. You're a dead man.'

'If there was a gaol in this town,' said Brown, 'I'd see you locked in it this night and then make enquiries to see what part you played in the murder of Aggie McDermott and Linton Avery. As it is, you're free to go, for now.'

'Give me back my gun, then.'

Brown couldn't help smiling at the impudence of the fellow. He said, 'I've been in towns that woulda lynched you for what you and your partners have been doing. Don't try my patience any further. Just leave.'

After Singer had gone off, presumably to see if he would be able to mount his horse and ride back to Parker's place with only one hand working, Brown said to his two deputies, 'You fellows want to take a turn up the road with me? I got one or two things need saying.'

When the three of them were out of earshot of the little crowd clustered round the four dead men, the teacher said, 'You two did better than I could have hoped tonight. I owe you both my life. It will not be forgot.'

Andy Porter looked a little embarrassed to receive such a compliment, but old Jack Brady merely nodded in acknowledgement. He knew that what Brown said was no more than the literal truth and took the thanks as his due. Brady said, 'That's the job only half done. Their friends will be lookin' for revenge. It ain't over yet, not by a long sight.'

'That's the truth,' said Mark Brown, 'But still and all, I won't ask you men to do any more. If you want to walk away from this now, I'll not think any the less of you.'

Brady snorted in derision. 'I ain't a man to leave a job unfinished,' he said. 'I mean to end what we begun this night. What about you, Andy?'

'You bet,' said the boy, 'You can count me in.'

'Andy,' said the teacher gently, 'You done right good tonight and I'm more grateful than you can know. But the next fight'll be a deal harder to win. I wouldn't feel easy in my mind about drawin' you into something which could be the death of you. You think carefully afore you say you'll stay with me.'

'I don't need to think on it much,' the boy replied, 'I've wanted to be a lawman since as far back as I can recall. This looks to be a good beginning. I reckon as you could help me along in that line, if I make out good now?'

'I'll surely do what I am able to help you, yes. Well, it looks like the three of us will have to see if we can settle the rest of those scallywags up at Randolph Parker's spread.'

Jake Brady scratched his head thoughtfully. 'You think they'll come tonight? Or you figure we can sleep now and be ready in the morning?'

'I don't look for them to be riding out here this

night. They're probably busy terrorizing some poor sodbusters right this minute. But they will want revenge for the death of their friends, that's for sure. I say you two fellows should go home to your beds and if you still want to help me tomorrow, we'll set off and see what we can do.'

Andy left the other two and went home, presumably to face his mother's wrath. As he walked down Main Street with the owner of the livery stable, Brown said, 'You were quick to offer your services to me, Mr Brady. How's that?'

'Fellow gets tired of tacking up horses and polishing leather all the live-long day. I was in the army when I was younger and after that, I was mixed up in some high jinks. Being an old-timer don't always suit a man, no matter his age. Just thought it might be fun to let rip again and see if I could still hold my own. 'Sides which, my health ain't what you'd describe as robust. I'd like to do what I can, while I'm still able.'

Mark Brown stopped walking and turned to face the other man. He said, 'You did better than hold your own. You and that boy are the only real men in this whole entire town. I don't know how old you are, but I'd sooner have you by my side than any of the younger men round here.'

The old man shook his head, saying, 'People in this town are all right. They just got a little soft is all. Things is easier than when I was young. Goodnight to you, Mr Brown.'

'Goodnight, Mr Brady.'

He would have to make some provision for the men that he and the others had slain that night, but suddenly the teacher felt bone-weary. Let those who lived in the town make arrangements. He was done for the night. Brown had a suspicion that the next day was apt to be a trying one, with him and the other two facing odds of around seven to one.

Mrs Clayton was sitting in the parlour, with only one lamp alight, reading a newspaper. When he entered the house, she called out to him. 'Come and set here with me for a moment if you will, Mr Brown. You might care for a cup of coffee.'

'That would be truly welcome, ma'am.'

As the old woman poured out the coffee, she said, 'Well, I heard some shooting. Not just pistols either, 'less my hearing is failing. I hope only the bad men were hurt?'

'Your nephew and Mr Brady from the livery stable are just fine. Not so much as a scratch.'

'What about you? You all right as well?'

'By God's mercy, I am.'

'Amen to that, say I. How many killed?'

'We shot four of the men who I think killed your brother-in-law. Another one is out of action.'

'Well, you do get things done, I will allow. Are you hungry?'

Brown thought about this for a second or two, before answering, 'Truth to tell, I have not eaten at all today.'

'Lord, that won't answer. I'd best rustle up something

for you. You sit here with the newspaper for a spell.'

Now that he thought about it, Brown was tired and hungry and the idea of sitting down and having a bite to eat was a tempting one. He settled into one of the comfortable armchairs, while the old woman bustled around in the kitchen.

She returned with a plate of sandwiches, which she handed to him. The teacher stood up, intending to take them through to eat at the table, but Miss Clayton stopped him, saying, 'You rest yourself there, now.'

As he munched the bread and cheese, Brown said, 'How's young Patrick bearing up?'

'Not so good. He's been sobbing a lot to himself.'

'Poor young devil. I wonder if I shouldn't take him to stay somewhere else tonight, ma'am.'

'Take him somewhere else? What, at this time of night? Why, you must have taken leave of your senses. He's snuggled safe in bed.'

Brown said, 'Miss Clayton, you are a good woman, but maybe you don't fully understand the danger. That boy is the only witness to the murder of his mother and your brother-in-law. Those murdering sons of . . I mean, devils, might want to silence him for good. Then again, they won't have any especial love for me after this night's work. If they come looking for me and find me here, then you could get hurt. I can't allow that.'

'Pig-headed young fool,' said the old woman fondly, 'You don't think you're the only one who knows his duty, I suppose? I want to see those men brought to account as well. I can't use a gun, but I can surely offer shelter to you and Aggie McDermott's boy. No, not another word. You stop right here until this business is over and done with.'

At about the same time that Mark Brown and Miss Clayton were having this conversation, Stuart Singer was arriving back at Randolph Parker's ranch. Riding with a broken arm was pure hell and the injured man had hoped to find his comrades in arms waiting to sympathise and help him plan his vengeance upon the man who had maimed him. He had forgotten that they had all drawn straws to see which five would get to go drinking in town that night. The other members of his party would be raising Cain around the nearby homesteads. So it was that when he eventually got back, there were none of his friends to greet him. A few of Parker's regular hands were around, but they all despised the newcomers as being little better than bandits. Not only that, none of the men who had worked at the ranch for years were any too keen on rebels and could not understand why their boss had chosen to engage such a set of bloodthirsty rascals.

Singer somehow managed to slither from his horse, losing his footing at the last moment and ending up on his backside. The jolt as he hit the ground was exquisitely painful for his injured arm. The men who heard his grunt of agony, sniggered.

'What are you laughing at, you bastards?' snarled Singer, 'I'll kill any of you who so much as smiles.'

The men shrugged and turned away, one of them

muttering audibly, 'Rebel scum.' Singer glared at their retreating backs. He picked himself up and made his way to the bunkhouses that had been allocated to their group; two log cabins, each containing half a dozen cots.

There were no lights showing in either cabin, and so Singer was forced to lift off the glass chimney of a lamp and strike a Lucifer with one hand. Then he lay down on his bunk and brooded of vengeance. His friends, meanwhile, were doing their best to persuade the stubborn settlers that the time had come to up sticks and move on.

Parker had told them that he didn't want anybody else killed now. The last thing he wanted was a bunch of federal marshals turning up on his doorstep, investigating a murder. The deaths of Aggie McDermott and her lover could perhaps be smoothed over as a bit of frontier justice. Any more killings would invite explanation. What he needed to do now was make conditions so unpleasant for those living hereabouts on his land that they would actually *want* to leave.

The eighteen Southerners who had not gone to town that night were busily trampling over sown fields and uprooting fences. When they had caused enough damage in one field, they rode on for a mile or two and hit someone else's farm. Two of the men carried stoneware flagons of lamp oil and this they sprinkled liberally over a cart and wooden shed. Then they applied a light and galloped off into the night.

This sort of hit-and-run attack was meat and drink

to these men, who had employed such tactics many times, both against freed slaves in the Deep South and then later on in the Mexican wars. They had no doubt that they would be able to clear this land and then pull down all the soddies and fences erected by these dirt-grubbing squatters.

Some time after midnight, the troop of horsemen rode back to their temporary quarters and were astounded to find Stuart Singer, lying on his bed with his arm broken.

'What the hell happened, man?' said one of the raiders.

'And where are the others?'

'They're dead,' Singer told them.

'Dead? What all of them? How?'

'You mind that milksop teacher who came by here a couple o' times? Him as was dressed like a parson?' asked Singer.

'God almighty, you ain't saying he did for 'em?'

'That he did. Him and two others. He beat the shit out of me, busted my arm and then killed Mathers, Thomas, O'Connell and Grant.'

Mark Brown woke before dawn the next morning and instead of leaping from his bed to start making preparations, he lay there quietly for a minute or two, getting matters straight in his mind.

Action had always been more attractive to the teacher than deep thinking, which was another reason that he had taken up the post at Barker's Crossing elementary school. He had been sure that it would provide him with a calm year; and plenty of time to consider the serious commitment which he was about to make. A year of inaction! Four weeks was all it had taken for him to drift back into law enforcement. He was still as deeply religious as ever he had been, but it was beginning to strike him that Miss Clayton had been right and that he would not make any sort of a priest. He was a good lawman, but perhaps he would only make a second rate man of the cloth. Mayhap he should stick to what he knew he was good at.

The sun was just peeping above the horizon when Brown rose quietly and dressed himself. It promised to be a fine day and he felt a twinge of sadness to reflect that one way or another, there would certainly be some violent deaths in or around Barker's Crossing before the sun next sank below the horizon. Still, he thought, that's none of my doing. I haven't set out to look for bloodshed. If those boys had just taken my advice and laid down their weapons when they was asked, there need not have been any killing last night. I don't see that it can be laid at my door. With this comforting thought, he made his way downstairs.

To Brown's amazement, Jemima Clayton was already up and at work in the kitchen. 'You must move as quiet as a mouse, ma'am,' he said. 'I've sharper ears than most, but I didn't hear you stir. Surely you've no occasion to be up at this hour?'

'You're likely to have a lively time of it today, Mr Brown, from all that I am able to collect. You don't think I'd let you venture forth with just a hunk of dry bread in your belly, did you?'

As she spoke, the old woman was frying eggs on the range which, despite the hour, was already warming the room. The good Lord alone knew what time she must have got up to light the thing and have the kitchen ready for a cheerful breakfast for him. Brown felt touched and said, 'I'm mighty grateful, but you didn't need to go to all this trouble.'

The meal which Miss Clayton set before him was most welcome and exceedingly delicious. Fried eggs, toasted bread, porridge with honey and glasses of fresh milk. When he had finished eating and was sipping a cup of black coffee, Brown said, 'Truly, that was the best breakfast I've had since the war ended. I feel ready for anything now.'

'Well, be sure to come back by six this evening. I'll have a good evening meal waiting for you then. Mind you're not late, now.'

Randolph Parker was up earlier than he had been for at least ten years. He had fallen into the habit of allowing others to do most of the hard physical work about the ranch and saw no reason to stir from his bed before eight or nine on most days. Today was different, though. His foreman had knocked on the door late last night, to tip him the wink that there was trouble in the wind. The man didn't exactly know the nature of the problem, but he had heard the Southerners talking of riding into Barker's Crossing in the morning and killing somebody. This was the last thing that Parker wished to happen. Once he had disposed of the homesteaders, his aim was to live in peaceful co-existence with the nearby town. As long as they acknowledged him as the important local figure that he was and allowed him some say in the running of the town, he saw no need for any friction between his interests and those of the town.

The truth was, Parker had had about enough of the two dozen men who had travelled here on his invitation. They had been well-paid and had done what was required of them. After the three deaths and the damage wrought last night, he couldn't see that any of those sodbusters would want to hang about much longer. Parker's intention now was to give his hired guns a handsome bonus and send them packing; back to the south where they belonged. The idea of them rampaging through the town was not an enticing one. They would queer his pitch if they got up to tricks of that sort. Already, he had heard from his men that the new boys were leaning on storekeepers and demanding their drinks for free in the saloon.

When he got up that morning, Parker simply threw on his clothes and snatched a quick bite of bread and butter; quite different to his usual leisurely and extensive breakfast. He decided to go over and fetch a few of the men who had been with him for some time, in the hope that they would be able to persuade Singer's friends to stay their hands and not make ructions in town. As he was leaving the house, Parker saw the

Winchester hanging on its hooks in the hallway and brought it down. Then he went back into the kitchen and rummaged around until he found a box of shells for it. He loaded the rifle and walked over to the bunkhouse where his oldest and most loyal men slept.

There were only four beds in this particular bunkhouse, it being more like a cosy home than a barrack-room. The men who lived there were already awake and dressed when Parker knocked on the door in a cursory fashion and immediately walked in. He was greeted with murmurs of 'Hey, boss!' and 'Morning, sir.'

'One of you men scoot over to Fraser's cabin and tell him to arm himself and come straight over here,' said Parker, not wasting any time on the usual social niceties. 'You men get yourselves ready as well.'

'Ready for what, sir?'

'Ready to stop those hot-headed fools from Texas. They have it in mind to ride on the town this day and engage in a little bloodletting.'

The men exchanged uneasy glances. The idea of stopping those Southerners from doing anything upon which they had set their hearts was not an attractive one.

Jack Fraser, Parker's trusted foreman, arrived; he was armed to the teeth with two pistols at his hips and a rifle in his hand. 'What's to do?' he asked.

'I don't want those new men of mine going to town and shooting the place up in search of that damned teacher,' said Parker 'I wouldn't mind seeing him killed, but I don't want a whole heap of blood being shed in Barker's Crossing. I want that we should hold them here and then offer to lure Brown up this way, so they can shoot him on the road.'

Fraser looked dubious. 'I don't see them buying that, boss. Once those boys set their sights on something, nothing'll hold 'em back.'

'I'm paying their damned wages. They'll hold back if I say so.' He looked round the room and said, 'You're none o' you yellow, I hope? You men work for me, or had you forget? Get your guns and come out now.'

With every sign of great reluctance, the foreman and four hands followed their employer out of the cabin and towards the two bunkhouses where the Texans were staying. All well and good for their boss to tell them that he was going to order those wild customers to stay here and bide his orders, but none of the other five could see that end being achieved without a considerable amount of violence. When all was said and done, they were cowboys, not gunfighters. Still and all, the mood the boss was in this morning, he looked quite willing to give any one of them who hesitated to help him, their marching orders. Others had been thrown off the ranch before for crossing Randolph Parker at the wrong moment. It struck the five of them that it was now a case of either going along with the boss now, or packing their bags and leaving at once.

It was clear at once that this entire enterprise was

not going to end well. When they walked across to the two bunkhouses occupied by the Southerners, it was to encounter a hive of activity. Two of the men were leading horses towards the cabins, while others were coming and going, bringing out saddlebags and so on. It looked for all the world as though the whole boiling lot of them were preparing to leave for good. Parker felt betrayed. He had wired funds to a bank in Texas to pay for these rogues to come up here and had then paid them good money in advance. Now it looked like they were about to dig up and leave. True, he had more or less decided to pay them off himself, either this day or the next, but that didn't mean that they could choose the hour of their going. That was for him to say. It was time for some straight-talking.

'The hell are you men up to?' bawled Parker angrily. 'You ain't about to leave, I hope?'

'You hope what you want, cap'n,' said one of the men jauntily. 'We done what you asked. I reckon we're all square here.'

'Just you put those bags back in the bunkhouse,' said Parker curtly. 'I'll be the one to say when your work here is finished. You go when I tell you and not before.'

The man who had called him 'cap'n' smiled at that and then spat deliberately in the dirt. 'I don't think so,' he said and, turning his back on Randolph Parker, he went back into the bunkhouse to fetch out some more of his gear.

Now when a man has been in the habit for many

years of being obeyed promptly and without further debate, it can be irksome in the extreme to have a man speak so; particularly when the conversation is taking place on his own land, just a stone's throw from his house. Parker stared, speechless, as the Texans ignored him and continued to clear out their things from the cabins. His foreman sneaked an anxious look at his boss, hoping against hope that Parker wouldn't precipitate a direct confrontation with these men. It was a vain hope, because the ranch owner strode forward and picked up a saddle-roll that was laying on the ground. Quick as a rattlesnake, one of the men whirled round and said, 'You set that right back where you found it, friend. Else you and me are goin' to be fallin' out.'

'I'm not your friend,' said Parker heavily, 'I'm your boss and you are my hired men. All of you, stow that gear back in the bunkhouses and happen we'll say no more about this insubordination.' It was a poor choice of words, the expression 'insubordination' putting them all in mind of various snot-nosed officers who had tried to push them around in the past. The men stopped shifting stuff and turned to face Parker.

'Best do as he says, sir,' said Jack Fraser uneasily, 'This ain't worth fighting over.'

'Yeah,' said one of the Texan's mockingly, 'You do as your lapdog tells you and set that roll down.'

In an absolute paroxysm of fury, Randolph Parker hurled the saddle-roll to the ground and turned his back, stalking across to his regular hands, who were standing in a nervous huddle. When he reached them, he whirled round, working a cartridge into the breech of his rifle and raising it to his shoulder, saying to his men, 'All of you, help me now to set these fellows straight and get them to put their things back in their cabins.'

None of the Southerners took to having the Winchester pointed in their direction. Even then, bloodshed might have been averted, if Fraser had not begun to raise his own rifle. As he did so, the other men at his side reached down to draw their pistols. It was enough.

The fellow who had addressed Parker as 'cap'n' drew his pistol with practised ease and shot Fraser dead on the spot. Parker then shot at this man, missing him, but killing the man standing next to him. Seeing that the shooting had now begun and thinking that they had no other choice but to fight, Parker's remaining four companions now commenced to fire at the Southerners, who returned the fire with devastating effect. The most that the four cowboys had ever shot at before this day were bottles balanced on a fence-post. The Texans and Georgians were all seasoned soldiers who had been living by the use of their guns for more than ten years.

The end result of the brief gun battle was never in doubt for a moment. Randolph Parker, who was none too popular with the men he had recently hired, was the next to die after Jack Fraser. Two of the Texans were killed and another two received trifling flesh wounds, before the shooting died down and all the cowboys lay dead, next to their foreman and boss.

'Son of a bitch!' exclaimed one of the wounded men, who had caught a ball on the outer, fleshy part of his shoulder. 'Did you see that bastard? It was like he wanted to die.'

Stuart Singer came out of his cabin and said, 'You killed 'em all? You get that Parker, I hope?'

'Yeah, he's dead as you like,' said one of the men, strolling over to where Randolph Parker lay stretched out, with half his head blown away. The man aimed a casual kick at the undamaged side of the ranch owner's head. Then he said, 'What say we see if there's aught worth takin' from that whore's son's house?'

This idea was met with general approval and the seventeen men sauntered briskly across to the big house and then set to ransacking it. They took silver coffee pots, gold cufflinks, ornate snuffboxes, framed miniatures, cash money and anything else that took their fancy. They were on the point of leaving when one man found the strongbox from which Parker had been wont to dispense wages each week. This proved to contain almost two thousand dollars, which meant that each of them received a little bonus of over a hundred dollars.

The gunfire had attracted the attention of the other men working on and around the ranch, but none of them were inclined to come and investigate. From the large number of shots, it was thought likely that the Southerners had cut loose and there was no percentage in going up against those boys. The cowboys just kept on working, although at a somewhat slower pace. They had a suspicion that nobody would be harassing them today and asking them what the Sam Hill they had been doing all morning.

Having thoroughly looted the ranch-house, it looked as though there was little more to keep them there. This wasn't the first time by any means that these men had turned savagely on somebody naïve or foolish enough to think that he had bought their loyalty. They knew very well that there was no sort of law within several days' ride of this corner of the Wyoming Territory, and calculated that by the time anybody got round to looking into the matter, they would be long gone.

Mrs Porter was most decidedly not pleased to find Mark Brown knocking on her door an hour after sun-up. She said, 'Mr Brown, Andy is my only child. Could you not leave him out of whatever plans you have for this day? Mother of God, didn't he do enough yesterday, from all that I hear?'

'Your son tells me as he wants to be a lawman, Mrs Porter. I can help him in that ambition. I've been a US Marshal for almost ten years.'

'Last I heard,' she replied tartly, 'You're supposed to be a teacher.'

Andy Porter had perhaps heard this disputing, because he came ambling down the hallway, carrying his rifle. He put his arm around his mother's shoulders and kissed the top of her head, saying, 'Don't fret, Ma. I can take care of my own self. I ain't a little kid now, you know.'

As they walked towards the livery stable, Brown said to the boy, 'You sure you want to finish this off? I'd not think any the worse of you if you felt you'd done your share. You done a sight more than the other so-called men in this here town.'

For answer, Andy Porter said, 'Can you really help me to become a proper lawman? Or were you just saying so to stop my ma from fussing?'

'I can help you. Once I tell some folk I know about how you handled yourself in this affair, I make no doubt that I can find you a post as a deputy in some town. Might be a long way from here though.'

'I'm getting to a time when I want to live a little way from my ma,' said the youth. 'She loves me dearly, but that kind o' love can choke you if you have it day in, day out. You understand me, Mr Brown?'

The teacher chuckled. 'Yes, I understand you well enough. Felt much the same when I was about your age. That's when I left my own ma to go to war.'

There was no sign of old Mr Brady at the livery stable so Andy suggested that they tried his house. Brown had no idea where the old man lived, but Andy volunteered to lead him there. They met Brady coming out of his front door. He was wrapped up warm against the chill morning air and seeing the warm coat and the scarf that was tucked round the man's neck, the teacher had a twinge of guilt. Helping a young boy like Andy to cut free of his mother's apron strings was one thing; leading an old man into hazard, just when he should be looking forward to a quieter life, was something else again. He said, 'Mr Brady, why don't you just stop at your stable this morning? Me and this young fellow can manage what's needed.'

'Huh,' said Jack Brady, 'Don't bother with that foolishness. I'm coming with you all right.'

'So be it,' said Brown.

CHAPTER 10

As they rode towards Barker's Crossing, one of the men said to Singer, 'You know where we can lay hands on this devil?'

'He's stayin' with some old woman. They talked about him in the saloon, don't you recall?'

'Not really. I only heard just a day or two back that there was any sort of law at all hereabouts.'

'He ain't really the law,' said Singer contemptuously, 'Not 'til that swine Avery as we hung, mixed himself up in the business. Brown, him that now claims to be sheriff, was only the teacher.'

'Teacher? That's a blazing strange occupation for a man to take. Yet he still managed to best you.'

'You better not go any further down that road,' said Stuart Singer coldly. 'He caught me by surprise is all. It'll not happen again.'

Singer was in the foulest of moods. Even with his injured arm in a sling, he was still finding it a struggle to ride at a normal pace. Apart from the pain as the broken limb was jogged up and down, there was the small matter of controlling his horse. With every jolt, his hatred of the man who had inflicted such suffering and indignity upon him increased, until by the time they had travelled a mile or so, his anger was at fever pitch. His friends recognized this and left him be.

The great advantage for the men riding down on the little town was that they had all known each other long enough that there was often no need for a lot of wearisome conversation before taking action. It was taken for granted that a man who had killed five of their comrades and badly hurt another should be dealt with as swiftly as possible. The odds of any action taken here rebounding upon them at some future date were remote enough to be disregarded.

Meanwhile, Mark Brown, Andy Porter and Jack Brady were heading up to Parker's ranch at a leisurely trot. Brown knew, and supposed that Brady did too, that this was a very delicate operation which could easily blow up in their faces. For young Andy, this was just an extension of the excitement of yesterday evening and he would cheerfully have ridden into cannon fire if the other two men had assured him that it was safe.

'I take it you fought in the war, Mr Brady?' said the teacher.

'Two wars,' said the old man. 'I was one of them as took on Santa Anna, more years ago than I care to remember.'

'Did you though?' said Brown. 'They say there was

some hot fighting there.'

'That's the truth.'

Andy Porter, not having any martial exploits of which to boast, thought to steer the talk round to the here and now, asking, 'We going to lay an ambush for those men or what?'

'I was thinking more of arresting them,' said Brown, 'I don't want any shooting, lests it can't be avoided.'

Brady said, 'You think they're goin' to put they hands up when they catch a sight of you? I don't see it for a moment.'

'Hold fast,' said Brown, 'I see a mort of dust being kicked up over yonder. Less'n I'm greatly mistook, I'd say there's a troop o' riders over the other side of that hill. Heading this way to, I shouldn't wonder.'

'What you want to do?' asked the old man.

'I should say that young Andy here had the right idea all along. If those men are the boys we're looking for, we don't want to meet them on the road, not where they're likely to outnumber us six or seven to one. Let's get off the track here and lay up in that grove of trees, up there on the slope.'

'We best move pretty sharpish,' observed Jack Brady, 'They'll be upon us afore we know it.'

The three of them spurred on their mounts until they gained the cover of the trees. Then they got off, tethered the beasts at the back of the little copse, and took up positions overlooking the track along which the riders would pass. They didn't have long to wait.

The body of horsemen came over the crest of the

hill at a smart trot. If he hadn't have known better, Mark Brown would certainly have mistaken them for a troop of regular cavalry. They had that disciplined look about them; quite different from a bunch of civilians. Set seventeen cowboys to ride from A to B and they will straggle along the road any old how, chatting, smoking and weaving about where they please. Not so these men, who came on in pairs, each pair precisely the same distance from the one before and after. Such discipline was second nature to these fellows, reflected Brown. Apart from the pairs, there looked to be a lone rider, bringing up the rear.

It was unthinkable to allow these men to proceed into town, where they might wreak the Lord knew what havoc. The teacher wasn't inclined to stand up in full view and hail them though, so he drew his pistol and fired a shot in the air. The line of riders reined in in a moment and looked round to see who might be firing at them.

Mark Brown cupped his hands round his mouth and called down, 'You men had better throw down your weapons. We have you surrounded.'

'The hell you do,' shouted back one of the riders, 'Less'n a good two dozen of you, you'd better give us the road.'

'I'm a peace officer and I'm telling you all that you are detained. Surrender your guns and no harm will come to you.'

The sound of laughter wafted up to the three men concealed behind the trees. Brown said quietly, 'You

142

fellows might cock your pieces. Those boys are going to start shooting directly.'

Meanwhile, the men below had been scanning the countryside and fixed upon the stand of trees as the only place where any attacker could be hiding from view. One or two with sharper eyes than the rest had caught a glimpse of movement and were pointing out to their fellows where they thought that the man who had hailed them might be hiding.

'Andy, are you ready to shoot one of those men?' asked Brown.

'Yes, sir. Any of them in especial?'

'No, any one of 'em will do.'

Andy Porter sighted down the barrel of his rifle and prepared to shoot. He hesitated, though. Last night, he had felt no compunction, because the others had begun firing first. Now he was being called to shoot first. The young man took a firmer grip of the rifle and took careful aim. Just as he had steeled himself to squeeze the trigger, Brown said, 'Hold fire. Listen!'

Sharp and clear, although some way off, came the metallic notes of a bugle. From over the same hill that the men on the track below had recently ridden, came a most pleasing and encouraging sight. It was a troop of US cavalry, perhaps fifty strong.

The sun came out from behind a cloud and in the sudden illumination, the shining brass buttons of the cavalry twinkled like stars. Seeing a large party of armed men ahead of them, seemingly intent on holding the road, an officer gave a shout of command

and his men all drew their sabres, which flashed in the sunlight.

The Southerners did not appear to be in the least degree disconcerted by this development. They at once wheeled round to face the oncoming soldiers. Rifles were pulled from their sheaths at the front of saddles and without any words being spoken, they began firing at the cavalry. At this, as though a spell had been broken, Andy Porter too began shooting; joined by old Mr Brady, who let fly with his shotgun. Brown drew his pistol and began shooting into the mass of men.

Their sabres might have been good weapons for close quarter combat with lightly armed opponents, but they were little use against carbines. Several of the blue-coated troops fell from their saddles, mortally wounded. But then their companions broke from a canter into a gallop and in the next instant, they crashed into the other body of riders. Then it was a confused mêlée, and Brown and his two helpers had to cease fire, for fear of hitting the cavalry.

It did not take the cavalry long to assert their superiority over the party of riders who had fired on them. Within a very few minutes, the shooting had stopped and those of the Southerners who had not been killed in the battle were disarmed and taken prisoner. When things had calmed down a little, Brown called, 'There are three of us up here. I am a sheriff and I have two deputies with me. Have we your permission to come down?'

'You come down, but keep your hands in sight,' called back the officer in charge. 'Let me see any sudden movement and it'll be your last.'

The three of them fetched their horses and very slowly led them down the hillside to where the soldiers were now tying together the wrists of the men they had captured.

The young major who was apparently in charge of the troop greeted Brown and the others cautiously, saying, 'You men mind telling me what's going on here and why these others attacked us?'

'My name's Mark Brown. I sent word to you people. You are from Fort Jackson?'

'That we are. So you're the fellow who invoked the Enforcement Acts? My colonel never was more surprised in his life to receive your appeal. We thought such things only happened a lot further south than Wyoming.'

'These men are what you might call leftovers from the late war,' said Brown. 'I've an idea that others might want them down towards the border.'

The major said doubtfully, 'Well, we can't keep hold of them indefinitely. They're not prisoners of war. We'll hand them over to the duly constituted civil authorities in these parts. I'll need an order from a judge. I dare say you know all this, if it was you who drafted that appeal to our commanding officer.'

The teacher hadn't given any of this much thought when he had sent Pete Cartwright off with that letter. His only concern had been bluffing the army into lending a hand against these men. He had given little thought to the mechanics of justice when once they were apprehended. Now though, the problem of what to do with these wretches was an urgent one. Brown thought for a moment and then said slowly to the officer, 'You know, these men fired on your column and look to have killed a couple of your men.'

'That is so,' said the major, 'I've lost four men and they're lucky my men haven't shot them out of hand.'

'They're armed irregulars, undertaking acts of war. Under the provisions of the Enforcement Acts, you could take them back to Fort Jackson and put them before a drumhead court-martial.'

'Could I, by God? There's a thought. But wouldn't we be poaching on your preserves in taking such a step? Surely, you want them to stand trial in your own jurisdiction?'

'I'll lay my cards on the table, Major. My case against these men is largely circumstantial, meaning that they might walk free from a court case, but I can persuade a judge that the murders they committed were part of a joint enterprise. You got the clearest possible case of a body of men, not in uniform, levying war against federal forces. Men have hanged for that in the south.'

'And we wouldn't be treading on your toes? We're only here to support you, you know.'

It irked Mark Brown to think that those scoundrels would not face justice for what they had done to Aggie McDermott and old Miss Clayton's brother-in-law. The logistics, however, of his taking more than a dozen men as prisoners and somehow looking after them and keeping them safe until they could be brought to trial somewhere for murder were simply unimaginable. At least this way, those men would probably pay with their lives and that was better than nothing. He said, 'Major, we are very grateful for your aid, and if you were to take those men and try them for crimes against the peace of the Union, that would be fine with me.'

'Well, that's handsome of you. Let's see how things stand.' Together, Brown and the major tallied up the casualties and counted the prisoners. Four troopers had been killed in the brief skirmish and six of the attackers. This left ten Southerners to be taken back to Fort Jackson.

'That's odd,' said the teacher, 'I coulda sworn that there were seventeen of those men to begin with. I remarked upon it to myself, because there were eight pairs and one man riding alone. Maybe I miscounted.'

'Well,' said the young officer, 'Ten living men is what I have now. There are some injuries, but nothing that would stop anybody riding a horse. Two horses will need to be maimed.'

Jack Brady and Andy Porter took no part in these negotiations, feeling rightly that Brown knew better than them how things might best be arranged. The dead troopers were slung across their horses, but the cavalry declined to be burdened with a half dozen dead rebels. 'They can rot by the roadside,' said the major.

At length, everything was sorted out in a satisfactory fashion and the column formed up, with the prisoners mounted on their horses with their wrists lashed together. Mark Brown addressed a few parting words to these men. 'You're a bunch of cowards and rogues,' he said. 'You make yourselves out to be soldiers or some such, but you didn't scruple to murder an innocent woman for money. I hope you get what's due to you now.' He turned away in disgust.

Before the cavalry left, Brown said to the major, 'You saved our lives there and no mistake. We're eternally grateful.'

The officer smiled and for a moment, he looked like a young boy. 'Tell you the truth, a bit of action like this doesn't come amiss from time to time. I'm damned sorry about the men we lost, but my boys have been cooling their heels long enough up at that fort of ours. A skirmish like that should liven them up a bit more than any amount of drilling on the parade ground.'

'I'll be sure to send word to your commanding officer, telling him how much you helped.'

It was with a sense of anti-climax that the three men made their way back to Barker's Crossing. They worked themselves up to such a pitch that they were all expecting death to claim them that very day. The one who felt this most keenly was of course Andy Porter. He was young enough to find any sort of fighting a welcome diversion and a bit of adventure.

*

Stuart Singer rode as fast as he was able towards town. He couldn't keep to the track and the rough terrain was sheer torture on his arm. He tried to maintain a canter, but was compelled by the agony of his shattered forearm to slow down to a trot from time to time. He had a real and genuine fear that he would pass out from the pain otherwise.

On the one hand, Singer had it in mind that he had behaved like a deserter; running out like that in the middle of the battle. But then again, he knew very well that the result of it all was that the Yankee horsemen would be sure to kill or capture every one of them. If that happened, they would never be revenged upon the man who had brought them to such a pass. Never had he experienced such a loathing and hatred for any man as that which he now felt for that mild-mannered teacher with a star on his jacket.

With all the dust being kicked up and everybody firing or slashing at each other with sabres or Bowie knives, it had not been too difficult to slip away from the fighting. All other considerations apart, he would have been little use in a battle, with the state his right arm was in. No, the only purpose which he could now achieve was to end the life of that damned fellow who had queered the pitch for all of them and sent his friends either to death or captivity at the hands of the Yankees.

As he neared Barker's Crossing, Singer tried to recall who the teacher was supposed to be lodging with. It was no good though; the name escaped him.

All he knew was that it was an old woman. Before riding into the town itself, Singer reined in, so that he could take his good hand off the reins and take his spare pistol from the belt where it was presently tucked. He had another minor grudge against the so-called sheriff for the confiscation of the pistol, which he had been carrying the previous night. He had had that Colt Army with him throughout the whole of the War for Southern Independence and then into the Mexican adventure. Now it was probably gone for good and he was compelled to fall back on this old thing. No matter, it would serve its purpose well enough for what he had in mind. Singer reached back awkwardly and pushed the barrel of the revolver into the back of his pants, where it would be out of sight. He wished to appear in Barker's Crossing in the character of an unfortunate soul who has been injured in some farming accident. He would just have to hope that nobody had got a good enough look at him in the saloon last night and recognize him for who he really was.

Main Street was probably best given a wide berth, and Singer rode at a walk down a little lane running parallel to the stores. A young woman was hurrying along in his direction and he took a chance and hailed her. Taking care to clip his speech a little and avoid his characteristic Southern drawl, Singer said, 'Hey, Miss. Can you help me?'

When she saw his sling, the girl decided that this stranger probably represented no threat to her. She came up to Singer and said, 'What can I do for you, sir?'

'Tell me now, do you know the teacher here? Party by the name of Brown?'

'Mr Brown? Why surely I do,' said Lily-May Cartwright, 'Though he ain't exactly the teacher anymore, from what I can see.'

'Do you know where he's staying? I have a message for him.'

'He's lodging over at Miss Clayton's house, but I don't think he's there right now.'

'Could you direct me there? I'm a stranger in town.'

'I could show you the way, if you'd like,' said Lily-May, 'It ain't far.'

'Oh, you're very kind, but I don't think it'll be needful. If you can just set me in the right direction, I'll be obliged to you.'

The little house looked just the sort of place where a maiden lady would be living, thought Stuart Singer as he approached the neat little clapboard property. He dismounted and led his horse round the back, where he could make a swift getaway when once he had killed that bastard Brown.

CHAPTER 11

Mark Brown and his deputies rode back into Barker's Crossing in a cheerful frame of mind. For one thing, they were all still alive, which was more than Brown thought likely when they had set off earlier that morning. For another, it had turned into a glorious spring morning, which would lift anybody's spirits. The former town teacher thought that he might be able to leave Barker's Crossing now with a clear conscience; it would be hopeless to try and stay on as an elementary teacher after all this. Miss Clayton was right, he probably wasn't at all cut out for a quiet life, either as a teacher or minister. Whereas as a lawman, he was hot stuff. Maybe that was his destiny.

Andy was anxious to get back home and reassure his mother that he was safe and sound. 'Yes, you cut along home, Andy,' said Brown. 'We'll talk tomorrow perhaps of how I might be able to help you in your plans for the future. I reckon we've all of us had enough excitement for one day. You take it easy now, you hear what I say?'

'Thank you for everything, Mr Brown,' said the youth earnestly, 'I can't tell you what this means to me.'

Brown shook his head and smiled. 'The boot's all on the other foot. It's me as should be thanking you for your help. If it hadn't been for you and Mr Brady here, this town would have been at the mercy of those savages. You've more courage between the two of you than the rest of the men in this town put together.'

After Andy had headed off home, Brown said, 'What about you, sir? You going home now?'

'I've a word or two to exchange with Jemima, so I'll tag along with you, if that's agreeable.'

'Yes, that's fine. If you don't mind me saying so, Mr Brady, you don't look too perky this morning. Are you ailing?'

'I'm an old man,' said the livery stable owner shortly, ' 'Course I'm ailing.'

As they came nigh to Mrs Clayton's house, Brown said, 'That's odd. Look there, the door's open. I don't see Miss Clayton and I never yet known her leave her door wide open so. You think something's amiss?'

'Wouldn't have thought so,' said the old man imperturbably. 'She's most likely beating her rugs or some such nonsense.'

The two men dismounted and tied the reins of their horses loosely to a fence running along Miss Clayton's house. Jack Brady was right – there was nothing to fret about, but all the same, Mark Brown loosened his pistol in the holster so that it would come free without the least resistance, should he have occasion to draw. It was as he opened the gate leading into the neat little garden, that Miss Clayton came out of the house. She was not alone. Behind her was the man whose arm Brown had broken the night before. He would have recognized the fellow's mean face, even had he not had his right arm in a sling. He had a pistol held to Jemima Clayton's head and the teacher was close enough to see that it was cocked. The slightest twitch of the man's finger would be enough to blow the old woman's head off.

'Didn't expect to see me again, I guess?' said Singer, 'Thought you'd dealt with us all, did you? You and your army friends?'

'No,' said Brown, 'I thought I'd not miscounted. I knew one of you boys had got away. You'd have done better to ride for your life. What brings you here?'

'I come to kill you. Only thing is, I can't make out if I should kill this old'un first. She seems fond of you. Might hurt you to see her killed in front of you.'

Mark Brown's blood turned to ice in his veins. This was the very thing that he had feared; that his actions would bring disaster upon this good woman. He tried to keep the look of dismay from his face, shrugging and saying, 'It's nothing to me if you kill her. She ain't kin to me. She's only an old woman I lodge with.'

'Take your gun out of its holster with your left hand and drop it on the ground,' said Singer. 'But real slow, you hear what I say?'

154

Very slowly, Brown reached down and drew the pistol, and let it fall to the path. If he was going to die, well then that was one thing. As long as Miss Clayton wasn't hurt, that was the important point. The man turned the barrel of the pistol away from Jemima Clayton's head and aimed it straight at Brown's face. He said, 'You ready to die?'

At that moment, old Jack Brady rushed forward with surprising vigour for a man of such advanced years. He charged straight at the man with the pistol, who fired twice into the old man's chest. As he did so, Miss Clayton moved away and Brown knew that he wouldn't get any better opportunity than this. He stooped down as quick as lightning and scooped up his gun, cocking it as he did so.

Despite having been shot twice, Mr Brady had managed to keep moving forward and was now grappling with the Southerner. The man with the sling brought his pistol down on the old man's skull and then looked up eagerly, ready now to kill the teacher. It was then that Brown shot him in the face. He cocked his piece again and shot the man in his chest as well. As Singer slumped lifeless to the ground, Mark Brown darted forward, catching Mr Brady in his arms as he too began to fall. 'It's all right,' the teacher told him, 'You're going to be fine.'

'Not hardly,' said Jack Brady and closed his eyes, dying in Brown's arms less than thirty seconds later. When he realized that the livery stable owner was gone, Brown had a childish impulse to curse and rage

against the unfairness of it all. He laid the old gentleman gently on the path and stood up. Miss Clayton
was watching him and he said,

'Are you hurt, ma'am?'

'No,' she replied. 'That skunk only arrived a minute
or two before you and Jake.'

'I'm so sorry I couldn't save him. He shouldn't have
died so.'

Miss Clayton said, 'I shouldn't worry too much
about that, were I you. You did him a kindness.'

'Ma'am?' he exclaimed, startled.

'He was dying anyway. He had a growth, a cancer.
Didn't you know he was in great pain a lot of the
time?'

'I saw him take some medicine one time,' said
Brown. 'I didn't know that he was that sick, though.'

'Medicine? That was laudanum. It was the only
thing that could touch his pain. Even that wasn't
working much lately. If he hadn't died fighting today,
he'd like as not have died screaming in his bed in a
month or less. It was better this way.'

The aftermath of the affair kept Mark Brown tied up
in Barker's Crossing for another month, much to his
irritation. Having decided that he'd taken a wrong
turning about having a vocation, he was eager to get
back to Louisville and see if he couldn't get back his
old job. He thought, though, that it would be a poor
show to ride off from this town until he was quite sure
that everything was more or less in apple pie order.

The one definite and indisputable outcome of the whole business was that the fight between Randolph Parker and the homesteaders was over for good. With Parker dead and nobody having much idea of the whereabouts or even existence of any family of his which might have a claim on the ranch, the remaining cowboys packed their bags and left after a couple of weeks. Nobody was paying them and there didn't seem to be any prospect of them getting paid further for any work they might continue to undertake. Some of the hands finished off the looting of Parker's house that the Southerners had begun and by the autumn, it was hard to believe that the deserted and ransacked house had once been the home of the most important man for many miles around.

'Well, Mr Brown,' said Miss Clayton, three weeks after all the excitement had ended, 'I guess you'll be moving on soon?'

'I will, ma'am. You turned out to be right all along. I would have made a pretty poor priest. Settling the hash of bad men is far more in my line. It's a thing I'm good at.'

'It's a pity, though,' said the old woman, wistfully. 'I've kind o' got used to having you around. I can see that you can't stay, but still and all.'

'You proved yourself to be the most important person in Barker's Crossing, ma'am. I'd think most everybody knows that now. I don't think you'll be lonely. Anyways, you have young Patrick to keep you company now. He's a fine boy.'

'He is and it'll be my pleasure to raise him. What d'you mean, about me being important? How'd you work that one out?'

'You kept on at me about my notions of training for the ministry. You egged on Linton Avery to appoint me sheriff, recommended your nephew and Mr Brady to me as deputies. Lord, without you pulling the strings in the background, things might have taken entirely a different course.'

Miss Clayton went pink with pleasure. 'Well, well, there might be somewhat in that. None of the men in this town had the gumption to see what was brewing, so happen I did poke my nose in somewhat.'

'And what a mercy that you did.'

At last, the arrangements were all made and Mark Brown's gear was packed and ready to go. He was travelling light and his trunk was being sent on separately to Louisville. He lingered over his breakfast that morning, oddly reluctant to leave, now that it came to the point.

'You're not taking Andy Porter with you?' asked Miss Clayton, as he sipped his final cup of coffee.

'Not right now. But I won't forget him. There's a boy who showed that he had what it took. He's got more courage than most in this town. To think that in the end it was only an old man and a green boy who dared to stand up and fight. I'd think the men in this place would be ashamed.'

The old woman shrugged. 'Most folk want to avoid trouble if they can. You know how it is. You sit tight and hope that somebody else will bell the cat, so's you won't have to.'

Mark Brown wasn't inclined to take such a forgiving view of the case. He said, 'Cut it which way you will, the men in this town turned out to be a set of cowards. I know it and so do they. Most of 'em can hardly meet my eye when I pass them in the street.'

The time had come and there was no further reason to delay. Brown had always hated long, drawn-out goodbyes and he wasn't going to get into the habit at this time of his life.

'Will you come down with me to the livery stable, ma'am?,' he asked. 'I'd kind of like to wave you farewell when I leave.'

Miss Clayton was obviously touched by this. 'Course I will, Mr Brown,' she said.

Together, the teacher and the old woman strolled along Main Street towards the livery stable, which was now under new management. When he had settled his bill, collected his horse and fastened his saddle roll on, Brown walked back down Main Street with Miss Clayton. It was a busy morning, and there were quite a few people on the boardwalks who observed that their erstwhile teacher was about to make his departure.

In his pocket, Brown still had the little tin star that had been given to him by Linton Avery. He took this surreptitiously from his pocket and held it, concealed in his palm like a card sharper. Without giving Miss Clayton any warning of what he was about to do, Brown clapped his hands together loudly a couple of times and called out, 'Can I have your attention, folks?'

'Whatever are you about, Mr Brown?' asked the woman at his side.

When he was sure that everybody near to him on Main Street was looking in his direction, Mark Brown announced, 'I'm sorry to say, folks, that I'm leaving town this day, which means that you will be without a sheriff to look after your interests. Howsoever, I've made provisions, so you won't lack a resolute individual who will keep an eye on your welfare 'til a permanent peace officer is appointed for this district.'

It was plain that the townsfolk were intrigued and wondered what their former teacher could be talking about. They exchanged puzzled glances, trying to work out who would be the temporary sheriff of Barker's Crossing. When he was quite sure that everybody was watching, Brown reached over and pinned the tin star on the front of Miss Clayton's dress. He said, 'You've this lady to thank for sorting out your problems and I'm sure she'll make a better sheriff than any of the men hereabouts, barring Andy Porter.'

There rose a murmur of indignation and Mark Brown knew that he was on the verge of outstaying his welcome in Barker's Crossing. He leaned over and put his arms round Miss Clayton, squeezing her hard and planting a kiss on her forehead. Then he sprang into the saddle, touched his hat in a general salute and trotted off along the road leading east.